INFECTED CITY BOOK 2:

NECROTIC STREETS

BORIS BACIC

Contents

Boris Bacic

JAMES

The street was quiet. James detected no movement whatsoever. He tried not to look at the dead body of the woman that Angela had killed, but his gaze drifted there nonetheless.

She was on her back, one leg tucked under the other, a hand over her chest, the fingers constricted with rigor mortis that was already setting in.

Don't look at her face, James told himself, but he did that, too.

Her mouth was agape, her eyes glassily staring at the ever-darkening sky. She was covered in so much drying blood that it was impossible to tell where the mortal wound was anymore. On the ground around her was a puddle of blood and bloody footprints leading away from it, each step leaving a weaker print until it faded entirely.

Jesus. That woman is dead. She was killed right in front of me.

James looked at Angela, who was still gripping the murder weapon. He had it in mind to turn around, bolt into the house, and lock the door behind him. Would they come after him?

Angela must have caught him staring because she met his eyes and said, "Hey. You coming?"

There was a motherly kindness in her voice. It was vague, but it was there, just enough to convince James to continue going.

He pulled out the garage keys from his pocket and pointed them at the door. Before he could press the button, Angela's hand was firmly closed around his wrist.

"No," she said. "No cars. Those things will be on us before you know it."

"We're in a lot more danger on foot."

Angela shook her head. "Don't argue with me on this, James. Travis and I walked from the center of the city all the way here. We've seen how things work. And if we run into a roadblock with those freaks on our asses, we're pretty much done for."

James looked at Travis, silently asking him if he agreed with that. His gaze said that he did. In the end, James knew that survival was in everyone's interest. If Travis and Angela had planned on doing something to him, they could have already done it.

"Okay." James lowered the car keys and returned them to his pocket.

"Good. Stick to the sidewalk. And be as quiet as you can."

Angela took the lead with Travis and James walking behind her. Angela's footsteps were quick and quiet, and James found himself having to go much faster than his normal walking speed to catch up to her. Her head swiveled left and right as she scanned the street for any movement.

The occasional popping sound exploded in the distance. This was punctuated by a faint, blood-curdling cry that echoed around the block. Sometimes, the screams were high-pitched. Other times, they sounded guttural, throaty, deep like something a wild animal would make.

The sound that really made James jumpy was the rustling. He'd think it was footsteps, only to turn around and see the nearby tree's branches rustling because of the wind.

"How far away did you say this checkpoint was?" James asked.

They hadn't even left his street when he asked that question.

"If we keep going in this direction, we should reach it eventually."

"Why'd you go all the way here from the center, anyway?"

"The cameras," Travis said. "They showed all the other checkpoints being flooded by civilians. Riots were breaking out, soldiers shooting people, that kind of thing."

"Jesus."

"Things went really south, really fast," Angela whispered.

"We were lucky to make it out," Travis said. "Actually, Angela saved my life."

The group went quiet in anticipation of Angela's explanation. She gave no response.

"I was being trampled by a crowd of panicking people," Travis continued. "She helped me up and led the way through alleyways."

"Were there a lot of those… crazies downtown?" James hesitated before calling them that because he still didn't know what was going on with them.

Travis gave James a despondent look. "You don't want to know."

James could only imagine the havoc that was going on downtown. People stampeding over each other; police and ambulance units' warnings and attempts to calm people down falling on deaf ears; the crazed people attacking the normal ones, killing them in violent ways; gunshots exploding in crowds; children's hands slipping out of their parents' grasp and forever getting lost in the crowd…

He didn't want to entertain those thoughts anymore. Instead, he decided to focus on the practical part that might actually be of use.

"What's going on with the people, anyway? What's causing all of this?" he asked.

"There are lots of speculations," Angela said. "Playing the guessing game will do us no good right now."

When they reached the T-shaped end of the street, Angela peeked around the corner.

"Get back!" she said as she quickly stepped back.

"What is it?" Travis asked.

"Freaks. A lot of them," Angela whispered. She crouched behind a fence and peeked around the corner again. She looked in the opposite direction and said, "No way we're getting past them. Let's try the other way."

She crossed the street while the two men followed her. James dared to look back in the direction that Angela had said was a no-go, and he immediately understood why that was the case.

"Fuck me," the words escaped his mouth when he gazed upon the street crowded with people.

Most were standing more or less still, not counting the occasional twitch, scream, cough, or flailing of the arms. Most heads were hanging down, but some jerked upward from time to time.

Some, however, were pacing around the street. Their slouching backs, jittery movements, undefined waving of the arms, and unarticulated sounds coming from their mouths reminded James of patients in an insane asylum.

James's breath hitched in his throat when he considered the possibility of being seen and the entire crowd breaking into a dash after them. It became apparent soon that the freaks' focus was elsewhere because none of them gave any indication that they saw the trio.

"Hurry up, will you?" James urged Angela. "I don't want to stay in their line of sight longer than I need to."

The feeling was mutual, which could be sensed from the tension in the air like a rope strained taut to its limit.

James would have breathed in relief when they broke the line of sight with the freaks, except the adjacent street was also crawling with them. James didn't even know so many people lived in this neighborhood. No, they probably weren't from here. They must have poured in from downtown.

"Shit," Angela muttered as she stared at the group of freaks off in the distance.

Travis and James stared at her, waiting for her next suggestion. It was clear that she knew what she was doing, and they were perfectly willing to let her take the lead.

"We're going to have to double back," she finally said. "Try and reach another checkpoint."

There was no arguing there. But that meant that they would need to go through one of the more crowded areas of Witherton.

James put a hand on her shoulder. "Listen, we should go back to the house and wait for rescue to—"

"There's going to be no rescue!" Angela's head snapped toward him so frantically that James recoiled. "If you want to sit on your ass, waiting for the useless army to come rescue you, fine. Be my fucking guest. I'm not going to do that."

"Calm down, Angela," Travis said. "We're just talking here."

Realizing that she lost her temper, Angela raised a finger to her forehead and then said, "Sorry. It's just… I have a daughter in Salem. I was supposed to go visit her today. And then this…"

"Hey, if she's in Salem, then, at least, you know she's okay," James said.

"We can't know that."

"Salem is a hundred miles away from here. I doubt they allowed this thing to spread to other cities."

"Well, we don't know if it's just Witherton or not. Not when they cut off our connection to the outside world."

Some silence, and then Angela stood up and said, "Okay, come on. We have to go back."

BEN

Ben packed only the essentials into a backpack because he didn't want to be weighed down. That included food and water, spare clothes, rope, a first aid kit, a flashlight, some batteries, and a portable charger.

"What else? What else?" he asked himself as he knelt above the open backpack next to the bed.

He looked up toward Melissa's side of the bed, and his eyes fell on the basket on the nightstand. It was full of cream products Melissa used every night before bed, painkillers that were there preventatively, hair bands, condoms, and a fork.

Yes, a fork. Melissa often got pretty bad cramps in her inner thigh at night, so she used the fork to gently jab the painful spot until the muscles relaxed. At least once a week, she'd wake Ben up with a yowl. He'd immediately know what was up because it was a specific kind of scream. He called it her "cramp cry."

He'd open his eyes to see her sitting upright and reaching for the fork next to her. The scream would sometimes grow louder before calming into a moan. Once the cramp was gone, she would fall right back asleep, but Ben would have trouble doing so.

The first two dozen times that it happened, Ben stayed awake with her while she massaged her leg. After that, he tried to ignore it and continue sleeping, which proved difficult with someone screaming right next to him.

Ben stood up, holding the strap of the backpack in his hand, and walked out of the bedroom. He went from room to room, looking for anything that he might add to his backpack.

This was the moment he was supposed to feel nostalgic. To relive important memories inside every room. Fleeting, private moments that bore no significance to anyone watching on the side but were priceless to the married couple that shared them.

Ben found himself feeling devoid of these emotions. It was just a house after all. Each room was there to serve its function, and that was it.

He didn't even want to buy it, but Melissa fell in love with it the moment they stepped inside, so he did it to please her.

It was a mistake, though, because they ended up having to pour buckets and buckets of money into renovations of the house—buckets they could have saved had they not rushed too much with the house purchase.

When he reentered the living room and noticed Melissa's orchids in the corner, he thought about how sad she would have been for them to pack and leave. That made him glad she wasn't here because the last thing he needed was to have to juggle packing, making a survival plan, and comforting her because she got too attached to meaningless objects in the house.

"I think I got everything," he said, impatient to leave.

As he zipped the backpack up, he couldn't help but think again about how naked he felt without a gun. If he found himself in a situation where he needed one and didn't have it, he would be very angry at Melissa.

He disabled the alarms, went outside, and locked the door behind him. Sure, he didn't care about the house, but it was still his property.

After careful contemplation over whether to use Stephanie's car or the Audi in the garage, he came to the conclusion that Stephanie's car was already damaged, so he might as well continue using it rather than messing up his own vehicle.

He stepped inside the car, threw the backpack on the passenger's seat, and turned the key to start the ignition.

***

He didn't make it too far out of the neighborhood. The farther he got out of Broadside and closer to St. Peter, the more the chaos in Witherton became apparent.

The part of Broadside that merged with St. Peter was overrun with dead bodies and crashed vehicles. Crazy people roamed the streets, pacing in random directions, twitching, slapping themselves, flailing their arms.

Upon seeing Ben driving past them, they went wild and screamed, chasing after him like dogs. They ran after him for a pretty long time, and they didn't stop even though it was clear they couldn't catch up to the car.

After a while, they disappeared from the rearview mirror.

Whatever was happening to Witherton was like a disease, and it was spreading fast. Just because Broadside was more expensive didn't mean it would be spared. It wouldn't be long before the sickness infiltrated the tranquil neighborhood and turned into the warzone that surrounded the rest of the city.

An overturned truck blocked half the street at one point, the other half riddled with crashed cars. It forced Ben to stop the car.

He was glad he didn't use his Audi because he'd have hated to leave it to rot in the middle of the street and so close to a neighborhood like St. Peter. If one of those crazy people didn't damage it, then someone from the neighborhood would surely steal it.

"Looks like I'm walking out of Witherton," he said to himself, not happy about the prospect.

It was better anyway, he realized. Cars only drew attention from those crazy people, and the road would probably become even more crowded the closer he got to the outskirts.

He was close, though. Once he was out of Witherton, things should become easier. Or so he hoped.

Ben grabbed the backpack off the passenger's seat and got out of the car. He put the backpack on as he listened for any sounds, far or close.

The wind howled, but that was pretty much the only sound that existed, which unsettled Ben. The only place in the city he was used to being this quiet was Broadside, and even then, some noises could be heard, like dogs in the neighborhood barking, distant car engines, occasional voices of passersby.

As if hearing Ben's concern, a pop echoed in the air. Then another two. Then silence once again. It wasn't long before that muteness was replaced by a distant scream, and that was when Ben realized why the silence had unsettled him so much.

The lack of noise told him the street was safe, but the chaos surrounding him contradicted that. It was like returning home to see the interior demolished and fearing that the burglar could still be there.

The screams were evidence enough—the danger was looming close.

Ben needed to keep his eyes open. He climbed over the chain-crashed cars and hopped over to the other side of the street. From here, he could see legs peeking out from under the overturned truck, the shins broken, a hint of blood under the vehicle.

Ben imagined the chaotic scenario that took place in the street. It must have begun similarly to what happened to him and Stephanie while they were stuck in traffic. People went crazy and started attacking others; drivers panicked and started crashing into the ones in front of them, and so on.

The truck driver must have been going at a pretty high speed to cause him to overturn like that. He probably swerved in one direction to avoid something on the road—either a car or a pedestrian—and then lost control of the vehicle.

Continuing through the empty streets, Ben listened to the sporadic screams, gunshots, and police sirens in the distance. He made pretty good progress, and that's when the view in the distance made him stop dead in his tracks.

"What the fuck?" he said aloud.

He blinked, convinced what he was seeing was just a trick of the light. Even after squeezing his eyes shut and opening them for the fifteenth time, the tall walls that stretched in the distance were still there. And right where the neighborhood of St. Peter—and the city of Witherton—ended.

They've quarantined the city?

"Military checkpoint." A deep voice across the street startled Ben, causing him to involuntarily ball his hands into fists, ready for a fight.

A senior man sat on a porch, smoking a cigarette and looking in Ben's direction.

"Sorry, son. Didn't mean to scare you," he said in his sonorous voice with a southern drawl.

He planted one hand on his knee and stood with a groan. The tip of the cigarette in his mouth lit up as he sucked on it. Ben only then noticed the shotgun that had been sitting in the old man's lap.

Damn you and your pacifist beliefs, Melissa.

But the old man wasn't hostile. Not yet, anyway. If he was, he already would have shot Ben.

"You headed outta town, ain't ya?" he asked.

"Yeah. That's the plan," Ben said.

The man pinched the cigarette between his thumb and forefinger, the embers blazing as he inhaled the remainder of it. He then tossed the butt on the ground and stubbed it under his boot.

"Well, 'fraid it ain't gon' be possible. As you can see right there, way's blocked."

"What is that?" Ben gestured in the general direction of the walls.

"You got cotton in your ear, boy? Military checkpoint. They is closing off the city."

"How do I get out, then?"

"You don't. The way there is crawlin' with them loonies. You ain't getting nowhere close. My family and I tried leavin' earlier. Almost got killed. I had to kill two of them to protect my daughter. Blew their heads clean off, I did."

"Dad, what's going on?" The front door swung open, and a woman poked her head outside.

She looked at the old man then at Ben. A look of skepticism contorted her face. The old man's daughter.

"Don't worry none, darlin'. Just talkin' to this 'ere man. He was 'bout to head on to that wall right there. Woulda got himself killed, he would."

"Oh," the woman said. The skepticism on her face morphed into concern. "Where are you from?"

"I live in Broadside," Ben said.

"Not too far from us. We're practically neighbors," the woman said.

Ben nodded, but in his mind, he disagreed. They were neighbors as much as New Yorkers and Oregonians were. Even neighbors were no longer neighbors with all the crazy stuff happening in Witherton.

"Listen, I just need to find a way out of the city. Do you know where I can go?" Ben asked.

"No way outta the city, son. Not 'ere, anyway. Might wanna try another checkpoint, but the city's probably crawlin' with the loonies."

"Everything okay?" A third person appeared at the door.

A man—and Ben immediately noticed his hand resting on something tucked into the front of his pants.

A pistol.

"Yes, David. This man is just asking for directions," the woman said.

The guy ogled Ben as if trying to determine whether he was a threat or not. He gave Ben a curt nod and said, "Best find a safe place to stay. It'll probably get worse before it gets better."

In other words, *get the hell out of our sight because you don't belong here.*

The remaining wisps of scarlet in the sky were quickly being replaced by an ever-darkening tint. Ben needed to find shelter before nightfall.

"Thanks anyway," he said, grabbed the straps of his backpack, and turned to go back the way he came.

He heard the people on the porch whispering behind him as he walked away. He was already thinking of a different route he could use when the woman called out to him.

"Hey, mister?"

Ben turned around to face them.

"Listen, it's getting late. We're about to have dinner. Wanna spend the night with us? It'll be safe.

Ben looked at the man. He must have been her husband. A look of disapproval appeared on his face, but he said nothing to reprimand the woman.

The old man's expression had turned compassionate. It was the face of a father and a grandfather, and a person willing to help someone in need.

Ben's eyes bounced from the shotgun in the old man's hands to the pistol in the husband's pants. These people meant no harm. The husband might not have approved of letting strangers in, but they weren't bad. They wouldn't hurt Ben.

"Sure. Why not." He smiled.

HEATHER

It was still early morning when Heather and Abby left the apartment.

The blood beneath the door reminded Heather that danger was everywhere, so she made sure the coast was clear by peeking through the peephole first. The blood on the wall in the hallway was still there with a brownish color to it.

"Remember, we have to be quiet," Heather whispered to Abby as she unlocked the door.

She locked the apartment behind them because she wanted to believe their lives would go back to normal soon. She didn't think of this as a farewell to the building, just a temporary departure.

Heather led the way, holding Abby by the hand. They tiptoed to the elevator; then Heather pressed the button to call it. They were on the fifth floor, and the elevator was on the first. As it ascended toward them, something upstairs crashed and clattered. Heather didn't want to think about what that was.

She looked at Abby to make sure she wasn't about to make noise. Abby was curiously staring up at the ceiling, her mouth agape.

The elevator doors opened. Heather let out a drowning person's gasp then quickly reeled Abby in, pressing her sister's head against her chest.

Oh God. Oh God.

She'd closed her eyes merely a second after the door opened, but the image of the elevator occupied with dead bodies sitting in a puddle of blood was vivid in her mind. She didn't see the faces of the victims, and for that, she was grateful.

Those are dead bodies. Dead fucking bodies. Right in our building.

Heather hadn't even stopped to consider they might run into dead bodies—and killed as gruesomely as on the news. How was she supposed to explain that to a seven-year-old kid?

"Sis? Are you okay?" Abby asked.

Heather realized she was shaking badly and holding the back of Abby's head pressed against her chest, not giving her the freedom to look around the hallway. Abby may have been oblivious to most emotional cues, but she could always tell when Heather was distressed.

"Yes," Heather said with a quivering voice. "Um… yes, I'm okay. We'll use the stairs. Just don't look at the elevator, okay? Abby, don't look at the elevator. Okay?"

"Okay."

"All right. On three. One. Two. Three!"

As soon as she began uttering "three," she let go of Abby's head and pulled her by the hand in the direction of the stairs.

"Just don't look at the elevator, okay?" The sentence was meant for her as much as it was for Abby. Her voice was frayed, on the verge of cracking.

She had been so eager to get away from the dead bodies that she descended the stairs too fast, causing Abby to trip. Luckily, Heather managed to grab her before she could tumble down the steps.

"Sorry. I'm sorry," Heather said.

Those were dead bodies inside the elevator, she had to keep chanting in her mind to convince herself it was real, and that meant the danger was real, too.

It felt so surreal. She knew people died every day, but to know they died so close to the place they called home, practically at their doorstep, instilled a sense of dread and vulnerability Heather hadn't felt in a long time.

Heather and Abby's footsteps resounded against the stairs as they raced down. She slowed down and finally stopped at the top of the stairs leading down to the ground level. This felt like the right place to stop. Something told her they would be seeing more and more deaths ahead of them the moment they descended the stairs.

That was why she needed to make sure Abby wouldn't put them in any danger.

"Abby…" She leaned in. "Did you look at the elevator?"

Abby shook her head. Her eyes were wide in terror.

"If you did, you can tell me. I won't get mad," Heather said.

"I didn't."

"Swear on our parents."

"I swear, Sis."

No need to press her further. If she swore on their parents, she was telling the truth. It was a simple but highly effective spell Heather used to get Abby to tell the truth. She could be denying something that happened in school, and the moment Heather asked her to swear on their parents, Abby would go mute and reveal that way that she was lying.

It wouldn't be too long until Abby realized that swearing on their parents was nothing more than an empty, verbal oath, as powerless as a prayer.

Besides, their parents were already dead. Swearing on them while lying couldn't do any more harm.

"Okay," Heather said. "Sis, listen. You might see some things out there that will look scary. You need to remember they are not real. It's all part of the game. Okay?"

"Like what?"

Blood. Dead bodies. Red-eyed people.

"It doesn't matter what it is. But if you do get scared, just remember it can't hurt you because it's not real."

"So, what should I do?"

"If you see something or someone that scares you, hide."

"But why should I hide if it's not real?"

"Because we want to win the game, duh."

Heather ruffled Abby's hair. It evoked a smile out of both of them.

"Okay, Sis. I'll do as you say," Abby said.

"And remember. Stick close to me, and be quiet. Okay?" Heather lowered her voice to a whisper.

"Can we still talk to each other?" Abby asked.

"Yes, but if I do this…" Heather raised a finger to her mouth. "It means we have to be very, very quiet. Even more quiet than usual, okay?"

Abby nodded.

"Good girl. Come on."

They descended the stairs. Heather peeked into the hallway. The exit of the building was in sight. Rays of sun fell through the glass door, luring Heather outside.

It was a trap. It may have led to a brighter place than the corpse-infested building, but the allure of that light masked the depravity of the city.

Footsteps pattered on the floor above, and that same feeling of vulnerability struck Heather again. In the apartment, she felt suffocated but safe.

Outside, both the suffocation and the danger existed on a nebulous scale.

And they weren't even out of the building yet.

As they got closer to the exit, Heather could see a distinct red handprint on the door, and more red on the knob. She wrapped her sleeve around her hand to avoid touching the blood. The door opened, and the first wisps of the cool morning air licked Heather's face.

Instantly, the sounds she'd been listening to the entire time for the past three days—screaming, crying, gunshots, explosions—amplified. The brightness of the sky stung her eyes, forcing her to squint. Abby shielded her eyes with her hand, blinking hard.

A familiar stench lingered in the air. Something sour, wet, and old. Heather compared it in her mind to the alley behind Wonder Meal Diner where the staff took out the trash.

Two corpses lay at the far end of the parking lot, and Heather knew she'd only been fooling herself. The danger hadn't been absent inside the apartment. It was simply not as close as it was out here.

Despite the dangers of Witherton, it felt good to get some fresh air. Heather could feel her thoughts clearing up and the panic that had seized her gut ebbing away.

"Come on, Abby." Heather motioned for Abby to follow her.

Luckily, they were headed in the opposite direction of the corpses, but Heather knew it was only a matter of time before Abby saw one of them. She'd do whatever she could to protect her little sister's innocence, but getting out of Witherton unscathed would be difficult.

"Can I lead the way to the car?" Abby asked.

"Shh. Quiet, Abby. Remember? The game," Heather whispered.

"Sorry," Abby whispered back. "Can I lead the way to the car?"

"Not today."

The parking lot of the apartment complex could hardly be called that. There were no marked parking spaces. Grass protruded out of the cracks in the concrete. Many of the parking spaces consisted of patches of dirt and pebbles beaten into the ground from constant flattening under the tires.

The parking was a maze of narrow driveways, on the side of which cars were parked, making the drive to a free parking space like trying to get through a minefield.

Heather found at least one new scratch on her car every month, and there was nothing she could do about it. Most complexes in Baldwin weren't occupied with surveillance cameras.

So, when Heather told Abby "not today" about her leading the way to the car, it was because anything could have lurked behind the millions of corners in the parking lot, and she didn't want her little sister to take the brunt of the ambush.

The squelching that came nearby caused Heather to stop and pull Abby closer. She definitely made the right choice not letting Abby go first.

"Ow. Sis, you're hurti—"

"Shh." Heather silenced Abby as she tried to determine where the sound was coming from—and what it was.

Wet, sloppy sounds behind one of the many rows of cars. It sounded almost like...

Like chewing.

Goosebumps tickled Heather's forearms as she shoved out of her mind the image of a red-eyed person gnawing on human organs. She pulled Abby in the direction where her car was parked. Just a little longer and they'd reach it. Once inside, they'd be safe. No way the red-eyed people could get in, right?

The squelching soon faded behind. Heather noticed that some of the cars were out of place, blocking the paths, crashed into other cars. They must have tried driving out in a panic.

The closer they got to Heather's car, the more unease squeezed her chest in a vise. More and more cars jutted out. Heather had the bad luck of having to park all the way at the back of the parking lot, which meant she had to drive through to the other end to exit into the streets.

She already knew she would not be able to exit the parking lot without damaging her car. She didn't care as long as she actually managed to get her and Abby out. She'd probably need to nudge some cars out of the way, but she could—

Heather stopped.

"Fudge," she said, a substitute she used for the F-bomb around Abby.

A cluster of cars packed together in the middle of the driveway like sardines blocked the only path forward. Heather's car was not far ahead, but there was no way she'd be able to get through the crowded vehicles. She'd need a tank to make a way forward.

"Fudge," she repeated, biting the inside of her cheek to stave off the scream building up in her throat.

Fuck. Fuck. Fuck. This complicates things so fucking much.

"Your hand is really sweaty, Heather," Abby said.

Heather sensed resistance from Abby gently trying to free her hand, but she wouldn't let her. Not here. Not with that chewing noise behind.

To convince herself there really was no way to get to the car, let alone use it, Heather scanned the crashed vehicles once more as if she'd spot a gap she previously missed. Already, the panicked part of her was subsiding, making way for the one that thought rationally.

It was as if someone else was in control of her mind when she contemplated the next steps.

We'll just walk to the military checkpoint. It's not too far. The streets are probably backed up, anyway. Besides, we don't want to attract attention.

"Sis? What's wrong?" Abby asked.

Heather looked down at Abby, and she swore she could see in those eyes intelligence that exceeded what her little face usually displayed. Those moments of lucidity that Abby sometimes displayed came at random and lasted for mere seconds before departing.

Heather knelt in front of Abby so that they'd be at the same eye level. It was something she did whenever she wanted to have Abby's undivided attention, and Abby came to learn that the gesture was important, so she focused.

"Abby, listen. We're going to have to go out on the streets. We're probably going to see some red-eyed people out there. Remember what the rules of the game are?"

"We have to hide."

"That's right. We have to hide. So if you see someone, doesn't matter if they have red eyes or not, you hide. And you don't ever come out until *I* tell you it's safe. Okay?"

"Okay, Sis."

"All right. You're doing good so far." Heather stood.

They returned the way they came, but the chewing sound was gone this time. Half of the gate leading out of the parking lot was closed, the other half blocked by an abandoned SUV. Maybe the universe was trying to give Heather a sign by not letting her use the car because, even if she somehow made it past the cluster from before that blocked the path, she never would have made it out of the parking lot anyway.

The universe was a master of irony because, the moment Heather and Abby reached the gates, a car alarm erupted from the general direction where the two sisters had been just minutes ago.

The incessant *beep-beep* attracted screams and footsteps, numerous and voracious, and Heather knew her assumption about her and Abby being safe from the red-eyed people in the car was wrong because nothing could stop such an unbridled fury and lust for suffering.

Heather pulled Abby into the gap between the SUV and the wall. They sidled out of the parking lot and broke out into the empty street.

The universe may have been a trickster, but it could also be merciful when it wanted to be. Had Heather started the car and tried to drive out of the parking lot, she would have attracted the attention of the red-eyed people.

And if that didn't, then bumping into one of the parked cars and causing its alarm to go off would, spelling doom for the sisters before the Sneaking Game even began properly.

Thanks for sparing us, Universe, Heather thought to herself as she and Abby distanced themselves from the blood-curdling screaming.

PIERCE

"They haven't seen us. Good. Looks like you were right, Pierce," Reynolds said.

They were standing at the top of the stairs leading out of the underground mall, peeking at the infected behind them.

When Pierce looked at Lincoln, he expected a look of disapproval, still angry that he didn't have his way at the rooftop—which wasn't the case. He had to remind himself that Lincoln was a soldier like the rest of them, not a high school student who threw a tantrum because life wasn't fair.

"Hostile ahead." Shepherd pointed to the other side of the street.

A man stood facing an ATM, his back slouching, his shoulder shuddering as if he was crying.

"He's just standing there," Murphy said.

"Oh yeah, I remember it being mentioned during briefing that they can go into catatonia," Shepherd said. "As long as we sneak past him, we'll be okay."

"We can take him," Murphy sounded hyped.

"Then I hope you're ready for a lot of work." Shepherd pointed forward.

More infected stood scattered around the street in the distance. Pierce counted five. Three stood still, and two were pacing back and forth across the road.

"Captain?" Pierce asked. Everyone turned to Reynolds, waiting for him to make the decision.

"We've already lost a lot of time. As much as I'd love to plow through these fuckers, we can't risk getting their attention," Reynolds said. "Remember what the general said. They move like a herd. Meaning: If one sees us..."

"…all of them will come after us," Pierce finished his sentence.

"We'll get off the street and look for a less crowded area. Let's move," Reynolds ordered.

So that's what they did. They sneaked past the infected in front of the ATM. The more Pierce watched him, the more the man looked like he was crying because the ATM swallowed his bank card. Then they turned left into Levin Street, which was empty save for a corpse splayed in the middle of the road.

As they walked past the dead body, Pierce couldn't help but look down. It was a woman, but the age was impossible to tell because the head was missing. The neck ended in a mangled stump, a wave of dried blood spreading away from where the head should have been.

Pierce imagined the woman getting knocked down and a comically large mallet smashing her head into nothingness. Where were the remains of the head, though? There should have been brain matter, pieces of the skull and skin, maybe an intact eyeball still attached to the optic nerve.

This looked as if the leftovers of the head had been picked up and recycled. Maybe they had. Who knew how these infected freaks behaved? The general had said it himself—intel on the hostiles was still limited.

They turned right, which put them on the general path toward Welco Labs. They still had a long way to go, though. Things would become worse before they became better because they still needed to go through the crowded parts of the city.

Would the city even be as crowded as Pierce remembered it being? Back as a kid, he had to hold his mom's hand tightly while going through Victor's Boulevard. Otherwise, he'd risk losing her in the crowd. But that was back then.

Tons of people like Pierce must have left Witherton every year. It was the only reason anyone grew up in this shithole—to get ready for the real world. It was like waiting for a prison sentence to be over so they could get out.

The only people who stayed were the basic ones who favored a bland life, had no ambitions, and would be willing to settle working for minimum wage at the syrup factory or slightly higher wage in one of the few offices that existed in Witherton.

Pierce could see from the various new, flashy buildings that had been erected that the city was trying to lure in new residents, but was it working? Maybe aside from the aforementioned people, residents from small, nearby towns would find a place like Witherton appealing. Witherton to them was what New York was to Withertonians.

"Captain. Look." Murphy stopped in his tracks and pointed.

Everyone turned to see what Murphy had seen.

"Jesus," the word left Pierce's mouth.

He'd heard it before seeing it.

Sobbing.

Inside a small clothing shop with the window broken out, cushioned among the numerous standing mannequins was a little girl, her face buried in her hands as she wept.

"Keep moving," Reynolds said, his voice barely above a whisper.

"We can't leave her there, captain. She'll die," Murphy said.

"You suggest we take her with us? Just shut up, and keep moving, Murphy."

"No."

"Excuse me?"

By then, the team had stopped walking. Reynolds and Murphy were facing each other.

"Look, let's at least warn her to hide. We can do that much. She's just a damn kid, captain."

Murphy had become a father only two years ago. His parental intuition was outweighing his military one. Big mistake.

"Murphy…" Reynolds started, but Murphy was already on his way to the shop. "Murphy! Goddammit!"

The team followed Murphy as he jumped through the broken window and scanned the shop with his rifle for any threats. Glass crunched under his boots.

"It's clear," Murphy said then lowered his firearm as he approached the little girl. She hadn't stopped crying, not even to look at who approached her. Murphy fell on one knee. "Hey."

Pierce didn't like this. He found himself white-knuckling his rifle, his finger ready to take the safety off and press the trigger.

"Hey, can you hear me?" Murphy asked.

"Murphy, let her go before she compromises our mission. Let's *go*," Reynolds emphasized the last word.

"Just a second, captain." Murphy raised a hand in a stop sign to the captain and then placed it on the girl's shoulder. "You're safe now. Okay?"

"Murph, forget her. Let's just go, okay?" Pierce said.

The girl's sobbing stopped. Silence filled the air, deafening enough for Pierce to hear his own heartbeat. The girl allowed her hands to slide down her face. She looked up at Murphy with puppy eyes, except those weren't puppy eyes.

They were bloodshot eyes, and the girl's face went from tear stricken and sad to twisted in anger. She bared her teeth at Murphy and lunged forward, a shard of glass brandished in her hand, squeezed so tightly her palms were bleeding. Pierce had no idea when she'd pulled it out.

In the end, it didn't matter how ready Pierce was because, when the time came for him to pull the trigger, he couldn't do it. He wanted to believe it was because gunshots would draw too much attention, but he knew the truth was he couldn't pull the trigger because the target in his crosshairs was a child.

"Shit!" Murphy fell backward, holding the child by the shoulders as she screamed at the top of her lungs and flailed the glass shard at him.

The room was filled with shouting as the team jostled forward to come to Murphy's help. Murphy threw the kid sideways with a loud grunt. She rolled across the glass-covered floor, knocking mannequins down. She was up on her feet right away, tiny pieces of glass embedded in her clothes and skin drawing blood.

The girl inflated her chest, and Pierce knew what was coming. Before her pent-up scream could reach an ear-splitting volume, a dull *thud* on the side of her head silenced her, causing her to topple like one of the mannequins.

Shepherd stood above her, the stock of her weapon ready for another smack if need be. The girl lay unconscious, the panting of Alpha Team the only remaining sound.

"Fuck me," Murphy said.

Captain Reynolds crossed the distance between them, and his fist flew across Murphy's face. A dull whack similar to the one the girl received from Shepherd's weapon exploded on Murphy's cheek, sending him stumbling backward.

"What the fuck!" Murphy held a hand against his face.

"What the fuck were you thinking?!" Reynolds was in Murphy's face. "You could have killed all of us, you moron!"

Murphy looked at the rest of the teammates. Then his gaze gravitated to his boots. Reynolds shook his head and said, "Let's move."

"Wait," Pierce said. "You hear that?"

He raised a finger. The screaming that perpetually filled the air sounded different than before. It was no longer isolated shrieks pinballing from one end to the other. It was an entire orchestra.

And it was getting closer by the second like a tsunami ready to sweep up anything in its way.

Shepherd's eyes flickered with understanding. The others knew what it meant, too. Just then, the communications radio crackled to life, and a tinny, urgent voice came through, three sentences that spelled out what the team feared.

"Alpha, they're on to you! Multiple hostiles inbound to your location! You need to get your asses out of there right now!"

DANIEL

Skinner had done a lot more damage to the bodybuilder than Daniel had initially thought. Who would have thought that 9mm could devastate the brain so much?

As Daniel stared at the body splayed on the examination table, he pondered what to go for first. Should he take a tissue sample of the brain? Should he open the man's chest cavity to see if anything was going on with his organs?

He knew that the odds of getting any answers from a dead specimen were close to zero. If he had a live one, he'd at least be able to monitor brainwave activities. Like this, he could only hope to detect something under the microscope.

Daniel didn't let that deter him from trying, though.

He snatched a scalpel from the tray next to him and hesitated for a moment, wondering what the others were doing.

The door to the lab opened, and Melissa walked inside. She was visibly calmer now, but stress accentuated the bags under her eyes.

"Daniel," she said softly as she crossed the lab toward him.

"Melissa," Daniel responded. "Are the others okay?"

"Yeah. Chief Skinner just sent an emergency message to HQ. He didn't get a response yet, but he assumes it just takes time."

"Hm." Daniel nodded as he turned the bodybuilder's head so that he could gain access to the bullet hole in the back.

"The company must have noticed by now that something's wrong, right? I mean, they're bound to send someone up here," Melissa said. Her voice was laced with worry, and Daniel knew she was looking for confirmation from him.

"It's best not to think about that stuff right now. We're alive; that's all that matters."

An indirect way of saying "no," although he doubted Melissa would read between the lines. She was a brilliant woman, but panic and stress dulled the mind, made it incapable of understanding even the simplest influx of information.

"What do you think caused all of this?" she asked.

"I don't know. Might be a virus or a similar contagious disease."

"Do you… do you think we're infected?" Melissa stuttered to get the words out.

"Possibly," Daniel coldly said as he dug the bullet out of the bodybuilder's skull.

The chamber clinked into the tray he'd placed under the victim's head.

When Daniel looked up, he noticed that same worry from before back on Melissa's face. His words had a lot of power in that moment. He could raise her panic to the height of clouds if he wished so, or he could lie to her to give her a semblance of reassurance.

But Daniel never was the kind of person to offer white lies. People always called him direct and blunt and, in some cases, an asshole. But was he really an asshole just for being honest? The insults that the people directed at him were a reflection of their inability to handle the harsh truth. That's why he never took it personally.

Daniel wasn't a psychopath, though. He wasn't direct because he enjoyed seeing people squirm. He was like that because he lacked the patience to dance around the rim in order to avoid hurting people's feelings.

Seeing the anxiety washing over Melissa's face made him regret his words. He stopped focusing on the victim and said, "Look, I'm sure we'll be okay. If Welco isn't doing anything, then the government is. This is bigger than just one company."

"Right. I'm just really worried about Ben."

Her husband. Daniel didn't know how messy it was out there, but from what Sharpe and Richard had told him, the entire town was crazy. Authorities were spread thin, trying to put out the chaos caused by the people who had suddenly gone crazy without an explanation.

Daniel doubted Melissa's husband was still alive unless he was at home and smart enough not to leave the place. If he was even a little bit like Melissa, then he was out there right now, searching for his wife.

Daniel couldn't tell that to Melissa. The last thing he wanted was to cloud her judgment, make her go out there on a suicide mission in search of her husband.

"I'm sure he knows how crazy it is out there," Daniel finally said. "I'm sure he knows you're safe in here."

"Yeah. Ben doesn't panic like me. You're right. He's probably home."

"Right."

"But he must be worried about me, too."

"Try calling him."

At that point, all Daniel wanted to do was get rid of Melissa so that he could work in peace. He felt sorry for her, but he didn't want to babysit her and make false promises.

"I already did. Line's dead," she said.

"Keep trying." Daniel smiled.

"You're right. I will. Thank you for listening to me, Daniel. You've always been a good friend."

That gave Daniel pause. The guilt that simmered at the edge of his consciousness made him regret not being more empathetic toward Melissa. If only she knew what went on in his head, she would have lost the respect she so obviously had for Daniel.

"Melissa?" Daniel called out when she was already at the door. She turned around to face him with raised eyebrows. "Would you like to help me with this?"

Melissa's eyes dropped to the dead bodybuilder. Daniel expected her nose to wrinkle in disgust and for her to give an aloof "no thanks." No, Melissa wouldn't say it like that. She'd reject the offer politely by providing an excuse as to why she didn't want to participate in the activity.

"Yes, I would love to," she finally said.

Daniel grinned. If he couldn't help Melissa in any way, then he could at least get her mind off things.

***

The offer to have Melissa help him turned out to be a good call because, just five minutes later, she was enthralled by the work they were performing. The focus she portrayed almost made it believable that there was no chaos outside and this was just another day at work.

Melissa was wearing surgical gloves, a face mask, and goggles as she stared at the open chest cavity of the bodybuilder. She gave Daniel a skeptical look. "Shouldn't you wear some protection? In case the pathogen is still active?"

"Melissa, every single one of us has been in close proximity to the insane people. If this was indeed caused by a microorganism, then I highly doubt any of us is uninfected." He lowered his gaze to the victim before Melissa could grimace under the face mask. "Well, organs seem unchanged. We'll have to make sure to do a biopsy in case we find nothing on the brain. Do you have the tissue sample ready?"

"Yes, Dan. It's behind you."

Daniel spun to see the sample ready to be viewed under the microscope. "Thank you."

He took his gloves off, threw them in the trash, and washed his hands. It felt weird following standard hygienic procedures in such an anarchic state. Then again, it felt weird dissecting a corpse, too. Daniel had only ever attended a real autopsy once during his college years, and back then it was an optional class for bonus points.

The memory of that class had been something potently etched into Daniel's mind. Standing in a semicircle with the rest of the students in the brightly lit morgue—because only in horror movies were morgues dark to give a feeling of suspense—while Professor Miller explained what he was doing every step of the way.

As a still-green twenty-year-old, Daniel could hardly focus on the cuts Professor Miller made on the young woman. He couldn't tear his eyes away from her pale face, wondering how she had died and whether her family knew a bunch of students were watching her dissection like she was a zoo animal.

Daniel later learned that the victim had been a drug addict who had OD'd. Throughout the following weeks, he kept seeing the woman's face in the crowd whenever he walked past girls with the same tawny hair and pronounced cheekbones.

Eventually, the experience faded out of existence—like a dream from years ago. That entire experience had slunk back to Daniel today and then faded just as quickly in comparison to all the dead bodies he'd seen in the past twelve hours.

Still, he was very close to feeling indifferent about all the death he'd seen today. He wanted to believe it was years of working in the medical industry that had desensitized him. In reality, it was probably his brain's defense mechanism protecting him by elevating adrenaline levels.

"Let's see what we're dealing with, then," Daniel said as he leaned to align one eye with the ocular lens.

He rotated the focus until the image cleared up. At first, everything seemed as normal as normal brain tissues could look.

Then he noticed the movement.

"See anything?" Melissa asked. She sounded like she was out of breath.

Instead of responding, Daniel fine-tuned the focus a little more, sure that he was seeing things right. Nothing. No movement. Just his brain eager to jump to conclusions.

"Dammit," he said.

"What is it?" Melissa asked.

Daniel straightened his back and turned to face his coworker. He opened his mouth, but before he could speak, a scream erupted upstairs.

JAMES

According to Angela, they would need to go through a crowded part of Witherton in order to reach the other closest checkpoint. If that one didn't work for them, then they would probably need to wait things out somewhere because it would be too dangerous to go for the remaining three checkpoints since it would require them to go all the way through downtown.

As they exited South Vale, things seemed to quiet down a little. Or maybe it was just their imagination. The animalistic sounds were still in the vicinity, but they seemed to have lost their potency and numbers.

On their way down Hawk Road, they decided to stop at a nearby gas station to take a break. Travis had been the one who insisted on it. The entire group was tired— from the long walk plus the exhaustion of having to stay alert the entire time—but Travis was worse off.

Whenever James looked at him, beads of sweat coated his forehead, and he seemed to be slouching more and more downward with each passing minute.

"Guess eating one meal and working twelve hours a day finally caught up to me," Travis said with a meek smile when he noticed James eyeing him.

"We've been on our feet for a while," Angela said. "Let's take a break in here."

A lonesome car sat next to one of the pumps. Something dark stained the hood, but no one was around. One of the glass walls of the gas station was shattered. The millions of tiny glass shards crunched under the group's shoes as they plodded closer to the interior.

Angela at the front, she held a flashlight in one hand, using the incandescent beam of light to scan the black interior, the ax firmly gripped in the other hand. James had taken the knife out of his pocket and was clutching it in his clammy hand, following closely behind. Travis seemed content with waiting outside while they scouted the area.

The inside of the gas station looked pretty much exactly the way James expected it would in an apocalyptic scenario.

The remaining shelves that stood had been stripped of most food. The floor was interspersed with bags of candies, chips, shards of glass, and in some places, blood stains. No signs of dead bodies, which James was grateful for.

He was even more grateful that there were no signs of movement other than their own.

"Okay. I think we're clear," Angela said. "Also a good time to stock up on supplies and take a break."

A soft crunch behind James made him twirl around with the knife raised at the ready for an attack.

"Whoa. Relax," Travis said atonally, a skeletal smile stretched across his face.

"Sorry." James sighed in relief. For a moment there, his legs cut off, and his heart began racing faster.

"Stop playing around and grab what you can," Angela said.

The backpack was in her hand, unzipped, and she was stuffing the remaining food from the shelves into it.

"Why don't we take a break first?" Travis suggested.

"Because you never know if something might force us to flee. We'd best be prepared."

Travis loudly grunted. As much as James himself wanted to sit down for a moment (It wasn't that he was tired; he just needed a moment to sit because all of this was too much for him), he agreed that supplies were more important.

Some bottles of water were left untouched, so he scooped them up into his bag. After all, water took priority over food. He downed the bottle of water that he'd brought with him to make room for other supplies. Travis had no backpack, and the only pockets he could stuff items into were shallow, so he didn't bother taking more than a few chocolate bars.

Travis and James were done long before Angela. She went from shelf to shelf, hand-picking each item and reading the back of it before deciding if they would remain there or go in the bag.

"Okay, done," she said at last when she zipped up her backpack and hoisted it over her shoulders again.

They then sat down and ate some of the food in silence. James's gaze kept shifting toward the broken window wall as he nibbled on the Doritos. He pulled out his phone and checked for notifications. Nothing. The internet was down, too. He couldn't even use his own.

On a whim, James entered the chat with Julie. He stared at her final message, a feeling of, not dread but sadness creeping over him. Julie was probably dead.

Dead.

That word felt so foreign. And yet, no matter how much his brain fought against the information, he had to come to terms with the fact that all it took was one moment, and then the people he knew could be dead. Just a few months earlier, one of James's old friends had suddenly passed away from liver failure.

The two of them had had a very casual interaction just ten days before his death. And then the next thing James knew, he was seeing posts on Facebook, on his friend's wall, saying, "Rest in peace."

James tapped on the final unsent message to Julie to try to resend it. It wouldn't go through.

"Worried about someone?" Angela's soft voice broke the silence.

He looked up at her to see her staring at him. She was sitting against the wall, her arms hugging her knees, the ax on the floor next to her. It was the first time since James met her that she looked like a vulnerable human being. It was the first time he realized that Angela, too, was a person with fears just like he was.

"Um… this girl I'd been texting. She hasn't responded in a few hours," James said, trying to make it sound as matter-of-fact as possible.

"She could still be okay."

"I doubt it. I was going to ask her out on a date this weekend, you know."

He didn't know what compelled him to say that. Maybe a part of him didn't want any inner thoughts to go unspoken in case he, too, met his untimely demise. Maybe it was Angela's caressing stare that said he could confide in her.

"Seems like this thing fucked up a lot of our plans," she said.

"Tell me about it." Travis huffed. "My vacation was supposed to start on Monday. I had a booked flight to Portugal."

"Portugal?" James raised his eyebrows. "I've never been to Europe. I always wanted to see the fjords in Scandinavian countries, though."

"I had a lot of business trips to Norway and Sweden. It's okay if you like freezing your ass off all the time."

"What do you do?" Angela asked.

"I work for a consulting agency. I sell products that no one can afford to people who don't need them."

"You seem to be doing okay, though."

Travis let out a chortle. "Ask my ex-wife how she feels about my job. And my kids."

"Angela, you said you have a kid, right?" James asked.

Angela's face went rigid. "Yeah. An eight-year-old daughter. Her name's Riley."

"You said she lives in Salem?"

"Yes. With her dad. He and I split up a while ago, and he got custody of Riley."

"I'm sorry."

Some silence, and then Travis cleared his throat and asked, "Why'd they give the father custody over you?"

Angela seemed to hesitate for a moment. James could see that the answer she was about to provide made her uncomfortable.

"I had no source of income," she said. "And... one time, he caught me passed out drunk while Riley was playing outside. That was more than enough for him to tell the judge I was putting our daughter in danger. So, they granted him custody. I get to see her every weekend, though."

"That's one hell of a drive every weekend."

"What can I do? My job's here."

"What do you do?"

"I'm a cleaner at Welco Labs."

Travis whistled. Even James was impressed because he knew how difficult it was to land a job at Welco Labs, even a position at the bottom like a cleaner, security guard, or gate opener.

"Nice work. If you don't mind me asking, how'd you land the job?" Travis asked.

"I'm studying pharmacy, and that's where I met a researcher who put in a good word for me. One interview later, and I got the job. I actually plan on applying for an internship there as soon as I graduate."

James couldn't tell how severe Angela's drinking problem had been, but she was a living example that it was never too late to turn your life around.

A sudden crash from somewhere in the back caused all three heads to snap in the direction of the sound. Someone was here after all.

Angela was already on her feet, the ax in her hands as she walked in a crouched position toward the source of the sound. Looking toward Travis, James noticed the businessman not bothering to stand up. Embarrassment bloomed in James's chest at the realization that two adult men were being protected by a woman.

He stood up and followed Angela to the backdoor. She stood in front of it, readying herself to barge inside. James gave her a nod of approval when their eyes met.

On cue, another clatter came directly from the other side of the door—something metallic hitting the floor and rolling until it halted. A part of James wanted to believe that the sound from earlier had been just an object left too close to the edge of the table or something. But there was no mistaking it. The tinny clatter confirmed that someone else was there with them.

Angela placed a hand on the crash bar. James held his breath as Angela readjusted the grip on her ax. Then, she shoved the crash bar forward and barged through the door, the ax raised above her head. James offered no hesitation when he followed her inside.

An effeminate scream erupted from the backroom. "No, wait! Don't hurt me, please!"

Angela's flashlight had been tucked into the front of her shirt, so it illuminated the room without her having to hold the small torch. Cowering in the corner of the small storage, on the floor, with his hand raised in front of him, was a young man.

"Please, please, don't hurt me!" he repeated, his shoes screeching across the linoleum as he tried to disappear into the wall.

Angela slightly lowered her ax, but not entirely. She understood what James did, too. This was not one of the freaks.

"Who are you? What are you doing here?" Angela asked.

"M-m-my name is Ricky. I-I work here at this gas station. I was working here when things started to become crazy. A group of violent people crashed inside. I think they killed my manager."

"And how did you stay alive?"

"I was taking a nap in here. They didn't know I was in here."

"I guess you were lucky you took a nap," James said.

"Tell me about it."

Ricky's hands were down, but he refused to budge from his spot. His eyes remained glued to the ax in Angela's hand. Noticing this, she lowered the weapon, allowing it to dangle next to her leg.

"And how are you feeling, Ricky?" she asked. "You feel anything… weird?"

"Weird how?"

"I don't know. Violent tendencies? Incoherent thoughts? Muscle spasms?"

"No, nothing like that. Why?"

"Did you happen to see what's going on out there?"

"Only from what I saw on the news before the internet went out. Things sure are crazy. I don't know what's going on, but I hope someone does something about it soon."

"I wouldn't count on it, Ricky," Angela said.

"What's going on in here?" It was Travis peeking over James's shoulder.

"Travis, this is Ricky. We found him hiding back here."

"Hi," Ricky said as he stood up and dusted off his rear.

"Huh. Surprised we didn't see him earlier," Travis said. "He could have killed us while we had our guard down."

"No, sir. I would never do that. I'm not a killer."

James felt a conflict brewing. Travis saying that he didn't trust Ricky; Angela rebutting by telling him that he was okay; James being caught in the crossfire, forced to take a side…

Nothing like that happened, though, because Travis simply turned around and returned to the main area. Ricky, Angela, and James exchanged quiet glances with each other.

"I guess it's time to move, anyway," Angela said.

PIERCE

"You need to get your asses out of there right now!" The radio man's voice was quickly drowned out by the ensuing screams.

There was no time to waste. Reynolds pushed the closest team member—that being Murphy in this case—toward the broken window. Everyone jumped out of the store and swiveled left and right.

The infected were coming from their left in large numbers. Dozens, Pierce estimated.

Pierce saw, even at this distance, how wild the crowd was. All faces were contorted into hateful grimaces as they sprinted toward Alpha Team, stampeding over each other, not caring that the ones that tripped were being run over.

Fingers and heads were being stepped on, but even as that happened, the unlucky ones on the ground kept raising their heads, trying to get up, still with the same, ravenous goal in mind—only to be knocked back down.

Worse than Black Friday.

Most of the infected looked like they'd been through hell. Those who weren't covered in blood or had limbs curved at strange angles were at the very least dirty like they hadn't changed their clothes in weeks.

"This way!" Reynolds shouted as he led the team in the opposite direction, back in the direction from which they'd originally come.

They dashed through the street, and… where to then?

Long before they reached the intersection, an infected appeared around the corner, skidding clumsily due to the inertia that carried him. Then another appeared. And another. Pierce recognized the third guy as the one who'd been standing in front of the ATM.

Reynolds leveled the barrel of his rifle with one of them and fired three burst-fire rounds. The ATM guy's left shoulder kicked back and then his head. Then he was on his back, motionless. The sound of loud gunshots made Pierce realize how real this just became.

"Move!" Reynolds shouted. "Get through them!"

More gunshots, not from Reynolds but from other team members. Infected fell, but more kept appearing in seemingly endless numbers, and the ones from behind were catching up fast.

Pierce ran, giving the infected a wide berth. They were dumb, which worked in his favor because he ran in one diagonal direction then suddenly changed directions and caused the chasers to lurch forward and hug the floor instead.

"Left! Left!" Murphy shouted when he reached the intersection.

Pierce only arrived there a second later, and when he looked left, he saw more infected coming from there. When he looked right, however, he was met with a few dozen more infected all running right at him.

Holy shit.

A tank wouldn't be enough to take them all down, let alone the four clips times five team members that Alpha carried.

More were coming from the street directly in front of them. Had they caught the attention of the entire fucking city?

Surrounded, going left was the lesser of the evils.

Gunshots reverberated in the air, but the cacophony of screams quickly suppressed them. Murphy was right in front of Pierce, the two of them running in line. An infected was running right at Murphy, his arms flailing above his head wildly.

Pierce slowed down just enough to fire a shot into the hostile's head. The head of the infected kicked back so hard his feet flew forward, and he fell flat onto the ground. Murphy stopped for a moment, poised to raise his gun at the already dead infected, and that moment was all the zombies needed.

An old woman collided with Murphy so hard that she sent both of them flying to the ground. How a brittle and small woman like that was able to move so fast and crash into a trained soldier hard enough to knock him off his feet baffled Pierce.

But there was no time to think. Instinctively, Pierce fired two more shots. The bullets hit the woman's temple, knocking her right off Murphy. Shepherd helped him up onto his feet, and then they were running again.

Reynolds and Lincoln were in front, shooting infected in their path, effectively clearing the way for the rest of the team. Lincoln darted into an alley. The captain stopped in front of it long enough to turn around and see whether the others were coming. When he saw they were, he disappeared after Lincoln into the alleyway.

Murphy, Shepherd, and Pierce followed closely behind. The majority of the infected were behind them with an occasional straggler trying to grab them before a bullet found its way into the attacker's head.

Alpha Team swerved from alley to street and then from street to another alley, then into another street. The hostiles were coming in endless numbers.

"It's no use! We gotta find shelter!" Lincoln shouted.

"There!" Reynolds pointed to a gated property with a basketball court and a wide building behind it.

Witherton South High.

Pierce knew the place all too well, but the last thing he had time for was reminiscing.

The squad hopped over the not-so-impressive mesh fence and sprinted across the yard toward the entrance. Pierce looked behind to see if the hostiles were capable of jumping over obstacles.

There weren't as many coming after them, he realized. They must have lost them during their zig-zagging through the streets and alleys. Just fifteen or so left.

The infected slammed their bodies into the fence, rattling it violently, clawing at the mesh, and pressing their faces into it. With the ones behind pushing against them in large numbers, the mesh began to slice through the skin of their faces, but they didn't seem to mind one bit.

Holy Christ, these things are abominations.

The fence posts began slanting under the weight of the infected clambering over each other. The fence wouldn't last long.

Pierce ran after his teammates. He caught up to them just in time when Reynolds kicked the front door down. He stepped aside to give the others time to get in. "Move it, Pierce!"

Pierce ran into the dark hallway so hard he collided with the far wall. He spun to point his gun at any oncoming hostiles. The doors closed just as the fence bent toward the ground, making way for the infected on top of the pile.

"Bar it!" Reynolds shouted.

Lincoln brought something Pierce couldn't see due to the dark and wedged it into the door. Reynolds flipped the desk that conveniently stood in the middle of the hallway and dragged it to the door, propping it under the knobs.

The muffled screams outside drew closer and closer and closer…

A loud bang resounded against the door, followed by growling. All unit members were pointing their guns at the door, waiting for the inevitable to happen.

The infected battered the door as if their lives depended on it, rattling it. Pierce glanced at the hinges, wondering how long they'd be able to hold out. He couldn't tell how long they'd been standing there, pointing their guns at the door, but eventually, banging turned into scratching, and the growling of masses receded into the moaning of an individual. Then that, too, stopped, and sweet, sweet silence remained.

But now they were faced with a new dilemma. They were stuck inside the school, and way off course.

"Here's the plan," Reynolds said, his voice strained. "We find a safe room to reload and catch our breaths. Then we go to the back entrance and get out of here. We'll find a different route to the doc."

Pierce couldn't shake the feeling that going through the school would be more difficult than facing the mob outside. No, he was letting his past cloud his judgment. The school was a ghost full of bad memories, that was all.

So, Pierce did what he always did when faced with his past—what he knew best.

He went back to being a soldier and focused on the mission.

JAMES

Ricky was more than happy to tag along. He had no intention of going back to what he called "his shitty excuse of a one-bedroom apartment on Broker Street." He'd mentioned that his parents lived in Vancouver, Washington and that he would hitch a ride there.

"What are you doing all the way out here?" James had asked.

"Attending UCS," Ricky had said.

"What's that?"

"You don't know?"

"Sorry, I've only lived here for a couple years."

"University of computer science. Pretty much the only good university that Witherton has," Travis said. "What's your major?"

"Artificial intelligence," Ricky said.

"They have that now? It didn't even exist until a few years ago."

"It changes all the time. By the time I graduate, the knowledge I've acquired from university will be useless, most likely."

"I'm glad I didn't choose computer science."

The veil of night gave the group good cover. The voices in the air boomed constantly around them, just like gunshots, and the occasional sounds of car engines, crashing, and screaming. After a while, the group stopped halting at every little sound that broke out.

And eventually, the screams became normal, no different than the howling of the wind. That, perhaps, worried James the most. The human mind was incredible at adapting to new situations until they became normal, but this sort of situation shouldn't be normal.

"We're approaching the city. It's probably going to become messy," Angela said.

Signs of how messy it was becoming were already showing. Cars were sitting abandoned in the middle of the road, crashed into each other or into houses and fences off the road. As much as James tried not to peek through the windshields, his gaze inadvertently bounced there anyway.

Most cars were empty, the doors left open, windshields cracked, airbags activated. A middle-aged man's head was slumped over the steering wheel, his head cracked open, his eyes staring emptily nowhere in particular.

James wondered if his neighbors had managed to get out. The road wasn't blocked by the piled cars, but he assumed that that would be the case the closer they approached Witherton's center.

Travis was starting to fall behind. The sound of his polished shoes dragging against the ground became more prominent. Often, Angela and James stopped to glance back at him. He was slouching more and walking under the street lights, James noticed how pale he looked.

"Travis? You feeling okay?" Angela asked.

"Yeah. Just… I need to take a break. Exhaustion's starting to get to me," he said.

"Sure. Let's stop here." Angela jutted her head toward an inconspicuous restaurant off the side of the road.

The group went inside and checked every corner to make sure the place was empty. The bartender's body was splayed face-first behind the counter, his head cracked open like an exploded pumpkin, blood and brain matter splayed all over the floor.

It wasn't until James laid his eyes on the body that the smell hit him. A faint whiff of metal invaded his nostrils. The stronger stench, the one of urine and fecal matter, was much harder to ignore. Ricky gagged somewhere behind James before adding something that sounded like "disgusting."

"Well, at least it's safe here," Angela said. "Let's take a break, and then we'll move on."

"I'm gonna use the bathroom real quick," Travis's words slurred from exhaustion as he shuffled in the direction of the restroom.

The other three sat around the only table that looked clean. James pulled out his phone, once again hoping for some kind of notification. Nothing. To make matters worse, he only had thirty percent battery left. His phone's battery was usually five or seven percent by the time he went to bed, so he knew that, by morning, his cell phone would be dead and he'd have no hope of contacting anyone.

Should have brought a charger, dumbass.

"So, I didn't want to ask too many questions earlier, but mind telling me now where we're going?" Ricky asked.

"Military checkpoint. We already told you that."

"Yeah, okay. I got that. But what is that, anyway? Are they gonna get us out?"

"That's what they said. They were organizing evacuation a few hours ago when this all started. I'm guessing they're still there."

"They might quarantine us," James said, a random thought that came to him out of nowhere.

"Maybe. But getting out of the town is our only option anyway."

"I heard they might nuke the city if they can't contain whatever this is," Ricky said, a little too perky for such a sentence.

"That's a little extreme." Angela frowned.

"Well, I know a guy who's in the Marines. He said that they just got an order to prepare for nuclear attack training."

"That's not how the military works," Angela said.

"Well, how would you know that? The guy I know is a lieutenant!"

"Because I served in the Marines for four years," Angela said.

That sentence shut Ricky up. His eyes widened, his mouth open, but he offered no rebuttal to that remark.

Now that James took a better look at Angela, he could see that she fit the profile of a Marine. The way she walked, talked, took control of the situation, remained calm... it all had given James a hunch that she had experience dealing with something like this, but he hadn't been sure.

His respect for Angela suddenly grew tenfold.

"Why'd you leave that lifestyle?" he asked.

"I wanted to focus on raising my daughter. The job made it difficult to do so."

"You ever miss it?"

"Some of the things. But I also like being able to wake up after six in the morning."

The group laughed. Even Ricky let out a nervous peal of laughter.

"Sorry. I meant no disrespect," he said.

"None taken." Angela leaned back in her chair.

The group went silent. A pop reverberated in the distance.

"Either of you have a gun?" Ricky asked.

James shook his head. Angela's reticent stare was answer enough.

"Maybe the owner of this place hid a gun somewhere." Ricky sounded hopeful.

"Even if we do find a gun, we're not letting you be the one to use it."

"That's understandable. I'd probably go firing somewhere I'm not supposed to, anyway."

Ricky's lack of counter-arguments surprised James, but he also found his quick surrender funny.

"Travis has been gone a while," Angela said.

James hadn't considered that until Angela mentioned it. She was right. It felt like a long time since Travis went to use the bathroom.

"I'll go check on him. I need to use the bathroom anyway." James pushed the chair back and stood up.

The chair legs scraped loudly against the floor, causing Angela to wince.

"Sorry," he said.

Despite the restaurant's pretty average design, it was visible that the owner of the place had invested a lot of money in the bathroom. Not only was it spacious, clean, and had motion lights, but the sinks and faucets looked unconventional.

Artistic was the only word that came to James's mind.

When James entered the bathroom, it had been dark. The lights turned on when he stepped inside. A hissing gasp caused his head to turn where the stalls ended.

Travis stood at the end of the restroom, facing away from James, staring up at the ceiling. The overhead lights revealed a bald patch on top of his head.

"Travis? You okay?" James asked.

Travis mumbled something that James couldn't understand. "What?"

He took a slow and steady step forward. Something was stopping him from walking up to Travis and grabbing him by the shoulder. Something that almost rooted him to the floor and screamed at him not to stay in the bathroom a moment longer.

"Travis," James called out once more, but the word sounded like it died in his throat before he even uttered it properly.

"Find the host," Travis gently said.

He remained in the same position that James had caught him in.

"Travis!" James called out, a little sterner this time.

Travis's head slowly lowered. Then, it turned to the side. James realized what was going on even before the next thing that happened. The moment he caught sight of Travis's violently spasming fingers, he knew that he was lost.

Travis spun around with terrifying speed and lunged at James with his arms outstretched in front of him. His eyes were bloodshot, a throaty scream escaping his mouth along with saliva that dribbled down his chin.

Before James could react, Travis had already collided with him. James's back hit the floor hard, knocking the air out of him. The back of his head whacked against the tile floor, a sense of vertigo overcoming him in an instant.

In all that mess, his body was considerate enough to tell him to keep his hands out in front of him for defense, which was a good thing because Travis was on top of him, thrashing and flailing his arms.

"Find the host! No control! Outside! Outside!" he screamed the nonsensical words.

His nails raked James's exposed forearms. His spittle flew out of his mouth and fell on James's face and shirt.

"Going! Going!" he shouted as he rabidly clawed the air in an attempt to reach James's face.

"Get! Off!" James hissed the words.

Then, a dull thud that silenced and froze Travis entirely exploded just above his head, like the sound of an egg cracking. When James opened his eyes, an ax was sticking out of Travis's forehead. The businessman's eyes and mouth were wide open in shock as if to ask, "Why?"

The blade that bit his forehead pulled out of his skull with a squelch. Travis's head made a jerking motion, and then he limply fell forward across James.

"Shit!" James pushed Travis off of him and scooted backward in a panic until his back hit the wall.

For a moment, all he could do was stare at Travis splayed on his back as blood trickled out of his forehead and down the sides of his face, pooling on the tile floor. Angela stood above him in a spread-legged stance, her chest heaving, the blade in her hand stained with fresh blood.

"Holy fuck. Holy fuck," Ricky said behind her, skipping from one foot to another, intermittently clamping one hand over his mouth and lowering it. He looked like he was about to throw up.

The burning in James's forearms reminded him that he had more urgent things to worry about. When he looked down, the abrasions on his arms were so bad they were bleeding. He also became aware of how wet his face and neck were with something warm and slimy.

He used his sleeve to rinse his face of Travis's spit, but the forearms filled him with despair that he'd never known before. It was over for him, and he knew it, no matter how much he tried to hide the scratches on his arms.

"James! Are you okay?" Angela stepped over Travis's body and got down on one knee in front of James.

James couldn't speak. A million thoughts raced through his head. Infinite outcomes but all tragic. Was he going to turn into one of them now that he'd been infected? What happened to the ones who turned crazy like that? Were they aware of everything going on while the virus controlled them? Or did they lose all consciousness while something else piloted them?

"Hey!" Angela shook James by the shoulder. "Talk to me."

"You guys need to leave."

Angela gave him an incredulous stare. James let out a sickly laugh and raised a scratched forearm in front of her face. "Look. He's infected me."

Angela stared at his arm for a moment then scoffed. "You're fine."

The sentence didn't make any sense. It raised a small feeling of hope inside James that he didn't like.

"But the virus…"

Angela shook her head before he finished the sentence.

"This isn't a virus. It's a parasite," she said. "And we all have it inside of us."

BEN

The house was nowhere near as ostentatious as Ben's.

The old furniture could have used replacing. The walls needed a fresh coating of paint, and the smell of cigarettes wafted out of them from years of smoking inside. The light bulbs emitted a diffused light that barely did anything to disperse the darkness.

The old man and the married couple weren't the only inhabitants of the house. When Ben entered, he was met with a scrawny woman smoking in the living room. The ashtray was full of cigarette butts. She jerked her head toward him and stared in surprise.

The wrinkles on her face said she was in her sixties. White roots were showing on her black hair, a testament to the fact that she dyed it. Thick, blue veins wormed down the back of her hand and her forearms.

"Uh, hello," she said with a grin, revealing rows of perfect dentures not common for heavy smokers.

"Martha, this is Ben," the old man said as he waltzed into the room.

What did he say his name was? Harry, right? Ben usually forgot people's names the moment he shook hands with them. The two young people he'd met earlier walked inside as well. David and Caitlyn, Ben remembered. They were married, and Harry and Martha were Caitlyn's parents, from what Ben managed to gather.

"Good evening, ma'am," Ben said.

Martha offered a forced smile but didn't bother getting up to shake hands or introduce herself. She went straight back to smoking the cigarette, and there was no doubt that, as soon as the current one was done, she'd immediately move on to the next one.

Stressed, it seemed.

"Go on, sit, son," Harry motioned to the couch as he waddled and took a seat next to his wife. He placed the shotgun in his lap, always so close to him. "Goddammit, woman. Will you stop suckin' on them poisonous sticks? You're smokin' up the whole goddamn house like a steam locomotive. You'll go an' make Caitlyn's asthma worse."

"It's fine, Dad," Caitlyn said.

She and David stood near the door. Ben felt like he was being watched for any sudden movements.

"No. She ain't s'pposed to smoke 'round you," Harry said.

"Oh, can it, Harry," Martha said. "It's been a long day. I think I'm allowed to smoke a little extra today."

Only Harry had that thick southern accent, none of the other family members.

He looked at Ben and shook his head. "You'd think someone would quit after forty years of smokin'. But she keeps comin' back to them like it's an ex-boyfriend she can't let go of."

"Oh yeah? Try being married to you for thirty-five years and see then how many you'll be smoking daily."

"Yeah, and you're the reason I went bald."

Ben thought they were arguing for real, but then he saw them smiling at each other.

"Thirty-five years and still not a dull day in our lives," Harry said as he put his hand on Martha's thigh. Martha put her hand over his. "I'd trade all my hair again for you," he said.

"Ugh." Caitlyn rolled her eyes, visibly cringing.

"Y'all gon' become like us, too. Don't think you won't." Harry turned to face David and Caitlyn.

"God, I hope not," Caitlyn said.

David was the only one in the room who stood with crossed arms, an impassive look on his face. From time to time, Ben caught his eyes drifting toward him.

"What about yer spouse, son?" Harry asked.

Ben pried his gaze away from David and faced Harry. "Sorry?"

Harry pointed at Ben's hands. "I see you got yourself tied down. But I don't see no woman in your presence."

He was referring to the wedding ring on Ben's hand.

"Oh," Ben said, suddenly realizing. "She, uh…"

He could feel all the eyes in the room on him. He thought about lying, but that usually meant having to create more and more fictional scenarios that would back up that lie. He was tired of doing that with Melissa and justifying himself with more lies every time he went out to see Stephanie—or the girls who came before her.

The world was ending, and Ben had no intention of spending what might be the final days of his life defending himself. Especially not to a group of strangers.

"I don't know where she is, actually," he said. The silence in the room was nearly palpable. "She works at Welco Labs. We lost contact earlier, and communications don't seem to be working."

"Welco Labs, you say?" Martha asked. "But that's all the way on the other side of town."

"Yeah." Ben nodded.

"Didn't you say you live in Broadside?" Caitlyn asked.

He already knew in which direction this conversation was going, and it made him wish he'd lied instead.

"Yeah. I do live there."

Caitlyn opened her mouth, a quizzical frown on her face, which drooped.

"I see," she simply said.

Why are you not going after your wife, that question asked. That question was poised on the lips of all the other survivors in the room. It was noticeable from the judgmental glares in their eyes.

"I'm just trying to get out of the city so I can get help. There's no way to get to Welco Labs. The city's all messed up. Especially the downtown area," he said.

"I guess if you went 'round next to Pearl Park, you should be able to dodge most traffic, but it would be a long, long way 'round," Harry said.

"Yeah." Ben nodded, his lips pressed tightly.

"Well, if I got separated from Caitlyn, the first thing I'd do is go look for her. Doesn't matter how many loonies I'd need to go through. Nothing would keep me from her," David said and gave his wife a loving look.

She reciprocated it. When she saw Ben staring, she cleared her throat and said, "Mom? Um, any news on the TV or radio?"

An obvious attempt at changing the topic but a very welcome one.

"No. Nothing still. Just the one about the military checkpoints," Martha said.

"What exactly?" Ben asked.

"Army's setting up checkpoints around the city. They're letting civilians leave through there," David said.

"And, let me guess. The closest one is where that wall is, right?"

"And there ain't nothin' getting close coz of the loonies." Harry leaned forward.

Ben rubbed his knee. "Maybe a way around, then?"

"Ain't gon' work. Too goddamn many of them. We tried gettin' there earlier. Almost lost our lives. There's gotta be hunerds of them, all just waitin' for some poor soul to get close so they could kill 'em."

"Well, I can't sit here and hope for the place to clear out."

"There ain't nothin' you can do, son. Not yet. Just give it a day or two, and somethin' is bound ta happen. The government ain't just gon' let us rot in here."

"I think that's exactly what they might do, Dad," Caitlyn said. "Waiting is a bad idea."

"Caitlyn's right, Harry," David interjected. "What if the horde moves here and surrounds the house? We won't have enough food and supplies to last us long."

He shot a glance in Ben's direction as if to remind him he wasn't welcome here. Ben's eyes once again flitted toward the pistol concealed in the front of David's pants.

"Well, there ain't nothin' we can do but wait." Harry shrugged.

"No. We can head to the other closest checkpoint," Caitlyn suggested.

"Sweetheart, that's miles away," Martha said, her tone condescending.

"Then the cathedral. It's closer."

Witherton had only one building referred to as "the cathedral," so Ben didn't need to ask which one Caitlyn meant.

"What's at the cathedral?" Ben asked.

"Survivors are gathering there," Martha said. "Not a reliable source I heard from, but it's better than nothing."

"Safety in numbers. We have a better shot there than we do waiting here," Caitlyn said.

"Well, we ain't goin' nowhere tonight. We'd best eat dinner and get some rest. Talk 'bout our plans in the mornin'," Harry said.

"I guess I should be on my way," Ben said as he stood.

He was already on his way to the door when Martha and Caitlyn called out to him, telling him he should stay for the night until he figured out what to do next.

Ben knew they'd offer to let him crash. Everything worked exactly how he hoped it would: him standing up and saying he should leave to give them the impression of not needing them. Then they'd offer him shelter, and he'd reluctantly accept.

"I really don't want to intrude."

"Don't be silly, son," Harry said. "It's dangerous out there. People is lootin' and killin'. It's mighty dangerous out there right now. Even the police can't do nuffin' about it." He said the word as *poh*-leece. "You'd do best to stay with us for the night, you would."

"Well, I mean, if you insist, I guess I can stay the night," he said.

He could see the look of disapproval on David's face, but he was in the minority. Everyone else wanted Ben to stay.

After eating lasagna for dinner that Martha had made, they showed him to an empty room where he would stay. It was a small room, the bed short enough to have Ben's feet dangling off the end. Empty aside from the bed and the junk that cluttered it, but it was obvious it used to belong to a kid. Probably Caitlyn, or her sibling if she had any.

Ben took off his backpack, placed it gently on the floor, and lay in bed, staring at the ceiling.

He wondered what brought Caitlyn and David to Witherton. Might have been just visiting her parents, and the insanity outbreak just happened to occur at that time. Such bad luck.

He wondered how David felt about that and whether he was mad at Caitlyn as much as Ben would have been at Melissa if he found himself stuck in a city, fearing for his life, just because his wife wanted to visit the parents.

But maybe David was different. Maybe he was the husband that would go through hell and high water to protect the ones he loved. Ben saw the way David looked at Caitlyn (while he wasn't ogling Ben like he was a thief). He looked at her like she was everything to him.

He looked at her the way Melissa looked at Ben.

Love.

The word always seemed so foreign to Ben. He knew what it meant, but he could never relate to the feelings that were supposed to come with it.

Butterflies in the stomach, the need to be with that person all the time, the protective instinct… those were all theoretical things, definitions in textbooks and portrayals in movies. For as long as he'd been with Melissa, he was convinced that he loved her, only in a different way. A way that transcended into something more mature, something beyond giving pet names and showing emotional affection.

Melissa always said she wished he'd give her more attention, but he told her it didn't come naturally to him. Cuddling and hugging her from behind while she cooked didn't necessarily equate to love, he often told her.

Everything that had happened today convinced him that he had been wrong. The emotion he'd felt toward Melissa wasn't love. Because when you loved a person, you feared for them. Ben didn't fear for Melissa as much as he feared for his own life.

No, it wasn't love.

It was comfort, and it was as far as he ever came and ever would come.

Still, he hoped Melissa was okay. For the sake of all the years they'd spent together. As for what would happen after this was all over? Ben didn't know. He couldn't afford to focus on what would happen after. Not while danger loomed so close.

Ben listened as the sound of footsteps and voices in the house gradually receded until they were gone altogether. It must have been past 1 a.m. by then, and he'd stayed awake the entire time. Even after the house went mute, he continued staring at the dark ceiling.

And when he was sure that everyone was asleep, he put his backpack on and left the room in search for firearms. If they had a shotgun and a pistol, they were bound to have more, and Ben was determined to find them.

DANIEL

Daniel had never thought about the quality of the building's insulation. He didn't need to.

Whenever he needed peace and quiet in his lab while testing samples, he had it no matter what hour of the day it was. No stampeding of footsteps or scraping of the chairs on the floor above, no muffled voices or laughter like back in his one-bedroom studio apartment on Creek Street.

The scream that had come upstairs prompted him to think that the company had cut corners when constructing this building. Either that or they went for appearance over functionality. The glass walls on the ground floor were proof of that.

"Oh my God. What was that just now?" Melissa asked.

Daniel clenched his jaw. He didn't need to speculate in his mind. He already knew what it was. The only question he had: Who did the scream belong to?

Without wasting time, Daniel broke into a dash out of the lab toward the source of the sound. Another jab of uncertainty hit him that the dead body builder would stand up and walk away while he wasn't looking. Just a nibble of a thought because the panic caused by the scream occupied most of his consciousness.

What would he find once upstairs? Dead bodies like the ones splayed just in front of the facility? His coworkers alive but crazy like the ones downstairs that were probably still pressed against the glass?

"Wait!" Melissa called behind Daniel.

But Daniel didn't wait. He climbed the stairs two at a time, tripped on one and almost fell headlong, and then continued running until he was on the next floor. He scanned the hallway left and right. Nothing in sight, which prompted him to resume dashing toward security.

He became painfully aware of how empty his hands were. Not even that meager scalpel to defend himself in case it became necessary.

For a man with an IQ of 141, you sure can be stupid sometimes.

He ran possible scenarios in his mind at hyper speed. Richard had become crazy like those people and attacked and overpowered Skinner. If that happened, it would be up to the physically unfit research team to put down Richard.

Again, Daniel would have to take the helm because Melissa was a small woman, and Sharpe was a man in his fifties that couldn't see his dick from his belly.

Dammit, why did it have to be Richard? He's the strongest of us all or at least looks like it.

The closer Daniel drew to security, the more dread crept over him like vines over an old house. He should have heard gunshots by now, right? So why hadn't he heard them? And then he realized why.

Skinner was running down the hallway to meet Daniel, his gun drawn. He wasn't at security? It didn't matter. A splash of relief hit Daniel in the face, cold but refreshing. Then, just as quickly, panic rose.

If Skinner wasn't the one who had screamed, then that could only mean—

Skinner turned sharply toward the corridor where the security office was. His shoes slid across the floor as inertia carried him before he regained momentum. Daniel couldn't keep up, but that was okay. Skinner was the armed one.

As soon as Daniel turned to follow the security chief down the corridor, he stopped dead in his tracks.

Christ almighty, he thought to himself at the sight in front of him.

He couldn't move. His brain screamed at him to do something, but his body refused to cooperate.

A patter of heavy footsteps caused Daniel to jerk his head at the sound, his hands defensively raised as a gasp escaped his throat.

Melissa came to a halt in front of him. "What's going on?"

She looked down the hall. Then her jaw dropped, and she muttered something—it might have been *oh my God*—under her breath.

"Step away from him, right now!" Skinner shouted, his gun pointed at the figure in front of him.

Richard stood in the middle of the corridor, facing away from Skinner, his head canted, arms falling relaxed next to his body.

At his feet on the floor was a figure splayed on its back, arms and legs spread wide. The huge belly stuck out upward hiding Sharpe's face out of view, the hem of his shirt untucked from his pants. He wasn't moving, and the garish red color on the floor that glistened under the overhead lights caused a knot to twist inside Daniel's stomach.

"Richard!" Daniel shouted as he stepped closer, but not too close.

He stood behind Skinner, a relatively safe distance from which he could observe the situation and have time to react in case Richard made any sudden movements.

Richard remained frozen in the middle of the hallway, a stance that unnaturally chilled Daniel. Something was definitely wrong with him. Otherwise, he would have responded to the loud voices—or the body in front of him.

Daniel's eyes had been glued to Richard so intently that he hadn't noticed Sharpe's face until it caught his peripheral vision. Then, he couldn't move his gaze from it.

The doctor's eyes stared vacantly at the ceiling. His mouth was closed, a trickle of blood coating the corner of his lips. Droplets of dark red marred his grizzled, prickly beard. His throat was a mangled mess of chewed flesh and exposed cartilage.

Oh my God.

"I told you to keep an eye on him!" Daniel shouted.

"I did! I was gone for literally just a minute!" Skinner justified, not taking his aim off of Richard.

"Oh God…" Melissa's soft voice said behind Daniel. "What are you waiting for? Shoot him!"

"No!" Daniel interjected.

Skinner's aim remained undisturbed, but his doubt washed over his face. He was contemplating whether to shoot Richard or not, Daniel could tell. Something had to be done before the situation escalated even more.

"What are you doing?! He killed Sharpe! Shoot him!" Melissa shouted.

So quick to pull the trigger. Easy for her to make the decision when she wasn't the one holding the gun. Would she have made the same decision had her husband been in Richard's shoes?

Daniel doubted it. He could picture Melissa throwing herself between Skinner and her husband, begging the security guard to spare him, even though she'd have no idea what she was dealing with.

Richard, on the other hand, was only a coworker. A person Melissa knew only by his name and face, who she saw five out of the seven days in a week, who she was forced to be on good terms with in order to make work more bearable.

Humans were hypocrites.

"Do not fire that gun." Daniel mustered all the authority in his voice for that sentence and hoped to God Skinner would listen to him. He took a step past the guard and said, "Richard? Can you hear me?"

Richard didn't respond.

"I want you to turn around slowly. Okay?"

Silence. The air was heavy with anticipation.

"He's not himself anymore," Melissa said. "We have to shoot him."

Daniel's eyes briefly flitted to Sharpe. The pool of blood that had oozed out of his neck onto the floor grew wider in the last minute.

"Richard," Daniel said softly.

Richard's foot shuffled across the floor in a rotating motion. Slowly, he spun to face Daniel, his head and entire upper body torpid, as if he could hardly bear his own weight. His eyelids were droopy, a thread of blood-mixed spittle hanging off his bottom lip.

Melissa's gasp momentarily distracted Daniel, but he remained focused.

"What the fuck," Skinner said when Richard faced them.

Blood drenched his chin, his neck, and the front of his clothes, as if he had vomited blood all over himself. Red wormed across the whites of his eyes, and his cheek twitched ever so lightly. A putrid smell emanated from him. It was the familiar stench of shit.

Did Richard shit and piss his pants after snapping like the crazies outside? Or was the smell coming from Sharpe, who had soiled himself in his final moments?

"Richard, can you hear me?" Daniel asked.

Richard's eyes were unfocused as they drifted from person to person like a sedated person unaware of his surroundings.

Daniel had to act fast. On the one hand, Richard could go wild at any second and attack the rest of the group just as he did Sharpe. On the other hand, Skinner's trigger finger was itchy. One side would inevitably suffer a death if Daniel didn't intervene.

"Skinner, whatever happens, do not shoot him. Understand?" Daniel pointed a finger at the security chief.

Skinner frowned at Daniel. *Are you out of your fucking mind?*

"Do not shoot him, you hear me? I want him—"

"Watch out!" Melissa's high-pitched voice tore through the air.

In that split second, Daniel noticed Skinner's eyes growing wide. By the time Daniel turned his head back to Richard, it was already too late. As Richard collided with Daniel with the force of a truck, all Daniel could think was, *He went from catatonic to rabid pretty fast.*

It made him wonder whether Richard had been pretending the whole time until Daniel dropped his guard. Daniel's back hit the wall hard, which knocked the wind out of him. Richard was in his face, his bloodshot eyes wide open and bulging like tennis balls, his jaw unhinged as he growled *haaa* in Daniel's face.

His breath was laced with a metallic and rotten scent, a smell that belonged to someone who had just woken up. For a split second, Daniel wasn't looking at Richard's face but the face of the woman in the morgue he'd seen so many years ago. He would have laughed at how much impact such a faraway image, even from the past, had on the human mind had he not been busy trying to stay alive.

Then he blinked, and the woman was gone, Richard's face replacing her. Except it was no longer his coworker. The person in front of him might have still been alive, but just like a drug addict who'd throw his loved ones under the bus when suffering from withdrawal symptoms, Richard was not in control of his actions.

Daniel pressed his palms into Richard's chest to keep him at bay. He cringed at the wet sensation of blood on his hands.

Richard's jaw snapped in the air like an alligator, his teeth clacking so loudly that it made Daniel's own teeth tingle unpleasantly. But even as Daniel wrestled against his crazed coworker, the thought that ran through his head was, *I hope Skinner doesn't shoot.*

"Stop! Richard!" Daniel shouted.

He could hardly hear his own voice from all the screaming in the hallway. Either way, telling Richard to stop was futile, as Daniel knew it would be. So why did he shout it, then?

Panic.

Before he knew what was happening, Skinner's massive arm locked around Richard's neck, and he yanked him down onto the ground. He squeezed his neck so hard that veins bulged on Richard's forehead, and his face turned red. Richard thrashed like a caged animal, choked, raspy gasps and growls coming out of his throat.

Skinner outmaneuvered Richard and got into a standing position. One precise punch to the face later, Richard was out cold.

Daniel felt weak from running up the stairs and wrestling. He had never been in shape, but being in his thirties, his already bad stamina was only worsening. He needed a moment to catch his breath and shout the one word that he was so desperately trying to get out.

The hallway was filled with heavy panting from Daniel, Skinner, and Melissa. Skinner pointed his gun at the unconscious Richard's head.

"Stop!" Daniel raised his palms.

"What?!" Skinner's head turned to Daniel, that same *are you out of your mind* frown on his face.

"Don't kill him," Daniel said.

"What?!" It was Melissa who had asked it this time.

"Are you crazy, doc?" Skinner asked.

"You don't want to kill him," Daniel said.

"Oh, but I do."

Daniel looked down at Richard. He looked like he was sleeping peacefully.

"Listen to me. Let him go," Daniel insisted.

Skinner turned back to Richard, white-knuckling the gun, his forefinger on the trigger and looking very ready to pull it.

"Skinner, you put that gun down right now!" Daniel commanded, even though he knew he had no authority over Skinner.

"But why?! He's dangerous!" Melissa interrupted.

Her meddling wasn't helping right then.

"Because we can use him to find out what's causing all of this!" Daniel shouted.

"You already have one specimen," Skinner said.

"Yes, but he's dead. Not a good test subject."

"And this violent thing is?" Skinner gestured to Richard.

"It's more than optimal."

"You're going to experiment on Richard?!" Melissa asked.

Daniel closed his eyes and focused on not snapping at her. "I intend on finding out if there's a possible cure for this."

Melissa seemed to shrink under his gaze.

"It's too risky." Skinner shook his head.

"It doesn't have to be. We'll tie him to the exam table. I'll do the rest from there."

"You can't be serious," Melissa said.

Daniel shot her a look full of venom. *Shut the fuck up, and let me handle this.*

Skinner looked unconvinced but open to at least listening to Daniel's suggestion.

"We probably won't get another chance to do this," Daniel said. "We can't let this opportunity go to waste."

Skinner looked down at Richard, then at Daniel, then back at Richard. He holstered his gun.

"You're really going to let him live?!" Melissa argued, but it was already over. Her words no longer had any power.

"Grab his legs." Skinner gestured.

Daniel already had blood on his hands and clothes. Getting a little more on him would make no difference.

It wasn't about scientific results. It was about saving humanity.

Boris Bacic

HEATHER

Morning quickly turned into afternoon. Heather had been sure that reaching the military checkpoint wouldn't take long, but she never went there on foot, so she underestimated the distance. It wasn't long before Abby started complaining.

"Sis, how much longer?" she asked.

"Not too long, Abby," Heather lied.

They were still a long way from their destination. They had managed to get out of Baldwin, at least, but the sense of danger did not diminish with that.

Heather didn't know what she expected she'd see outside of the neighborhood. A magical barrier that separated the post-apocalyptic Baldwin from the rest of the neighborhoods, maybe? She felt foolish for thinking she and Abby would be safer outside of Baldwin.

For the first hour of walking, Heather couldn't shake the feeling that, with every step they took, they were putting themselves in bigger danger because every step took them farther away from home. But then Heather remembered the corpses inside the elevator and the crashing and footsteps that resounded, and she knew the building gave only a veil of safety.

All around them were screams, gunshots, and noises that sounded like something wild animals would make. Heather could see the curiosity—curiosity, not fear—on Abby's face, so she explained to her it was all a part of the game.

As they walked farther, perpetual growls and grunts invaded the air, an unceasing cacophony of a plethora of people. It was difficult to tell where it was coming from, but the route the sisters would take was clear—as far from the crowd as possible.

"My feet hurt," Abby said.

"I know. We'll take a break soon, okay?"

"You said that earlier!"

"Shhh. Abby, we're still playing the game, remember?"

"This game is stupid."

"You wouldn't think so if you knew what the rewards are."

"Well, tell me. What are the rewards?"

"You'll have to see when we win."

Abby hung her head down for a moment then stomped one foot on the ground. "That's not fair!"

"Abby!" Heather stopped and leaned toward Abby. "What did I say about being quiet?"

Abby's arms swayed back and forth.

"I don't like this game," she said.

"I know. But trust me. When we win, you're going to be really, really glad we played it."

Abby looked like she was weighing whether to believe Heather or not. If she decided not to play the game anymore, Heather would have a lot of trouble convincing her to change her mind. She got that stubbornness from Dad.

"Here, tell you what." Heather put a hand on Abby's shoulder. "Why don't we find a place to take a break and eat something? We can continue the game when you're rested. Okay?"

"Okay," Abby said.

"But remember. We still have to be quiet." Heather lowered her voice again to show Abby how to speak.

Abby nodded.

They went on, but the orchestra of growls from before grew louder. They were getting closer.

Heather held Abby's hand tightly, her head swiveling constantly left and right as she scanned the street for any dangers.

"Look, there's a person." Abby pointed across the street.

Heather quickly blocked Abby's line of sight to stop her from seeing the corpse with the cracked head on the sidewalk.

"Don't look over there, Abby," she said as she forced them to increase their pace.

"Why? I'm not scared."

"Just don't look."

They slunk forward until the body was out of view. That was when they slowed down again. Unfortunately, more corpses came into view after that, and the number seemed to increase the more they traveled the streets. It was pointless keeping Abby's eyes closed.

It was stupid to think she could shield Abby from witnessing the violence in Witherton. But as long as they ran only into corpses, it would be fine. It was the people that worried Heather.

"It's all fake, remember? It can't hurt you," Heather said.

"I know, Sis. I'm not scared." Abby squeezed Heather's hand as if to confirm she was okay.

You're a lot braver than me, Heather thought to herself.

They were about to merge onto the street that would put them directly on the path to the checkpoint, but upon peeking behind the corner, Heather quickly retreated, a small gasp huffing from her mouth.

People.

Dozens of people occupied the street, pacing in random directions, blocking the path. There was no way through, which meant they would need to keep looking for a detour.

"We need to go back this way, Abby." Heather pointed the way they came.

"Why?" Abby asked.

"Because there are people over there, and we can't let them see us."

"Are they red-eyed people?"

"Yes."

Heather didn't actually know if they were red-eyed because they had been too far away, but the jittery movement, the random pacing, and the sounds they were making all told her that was the case because it was the same kind of behavior shown on the news.

They had to walk past the same corpses again. Abby was falling behind because she was glancing at the dead bodies this time.

"They look just like in that movie," Abby said.

She was referring to an old slasher that played on TV once. Heather had wanted to take a long, undisturbed bath, so she turned on the TV for Abby and told her she could choose what she wanted to watch. It was 6 p.m. Who in the hell played slashers at 6 p.m.?

The sounds of screaming mixed with the creepy violins in the background got Heather racing out of a bathtub with a towel wrapped around her. She tracked water all over the apartment, and when she entered the living room, she found Abby sitting on the floor, two feet away from the TV, staring wide-eyed at the screen that illuminated her face.

The camera depicted corpses mutilated in various colorful ways, blood and guts spread everywhere. Heather quickly grabbed the remote and turned it off, which turned into hysterics on Abby's end. The long, relaxing bath turned into a yelling contest between the two of them.

"Don't look at them, Abby," Heather said when they ran past the corpses.

For a split second, she felt like she was possessed by their mom because she used to say the exact same thing when Heather saw disabled people in public.

Don't look at them, Heather, and she would gently pull Heather's chin in the opposite direction.

Abby complied and picked up her pace.

"How do they make them look like that?" she asked.

"What?"

"How do they make the dead people look like in the movies?"

"Um… some special makeup."

"Cool. Can you make me look like a dead person, too?"

"Some other time, okay?"

It wasn't long before Abby started complaining again about her feet hurting and the game being stupid. Heather knew Abby was reaching her limits, so they had to find a place to take a break before she started screaming and crying.

"Okay, let's take a break. In here, all right?" She pointed to the closest open place she saw.

It happened to be a sports betting place. It was trashed to hell but empty, and that was the only criteria Heather cared about. It was also quiet, which was a welcome plus.

"You can sit or lie down wherever you want," Heather said as she slid the straps of her school bag off her shoulders.

It felt so heavenly to have the bite of the straps off of her. She allowed the school bag to fall to the floor and sat on one of the chairs that hadn't been toppled.

"But I'll get my clothes dirty," Abby said.

"It's okay. You can get dirty today. Don't worry about it at all."

"Can I play with my puzzle?"

"Yes."

"Yay."

Abby took off her bag, sat on the floor, and got the annoying puzzle out. Heather stared at her as she poured all the pieces onto the ground and began putting them together. With the feeling of caution fading for the moment, other emotions wiggled their way into the back of Heather's mind.

That same resentment that plagued her so often returned at full force, and Heather had no desire to dispel it.

Everything that was happening to Heather was because of Abby. She wasn't even supposed to be here, and even if she was, it'd be a lot easier for her to sneak around without an autistic kid weighing her down.

She stared at the little girl playing with that stupid, fucking puzzle, and she realized how much she hated her.

Yes, she *hated* her, and she was tired of pretending otherwise. She fucking *hated* her guts so much she sometimes wanted to slap her until her hand hurt. It felt so good to let those emotions rip. She'd bottled them up for so long, and she was sick of doing so.

All her life, she kept listening to *she's your sister so you have to love her as she is* and everything that happened was to accommodate Abby's condition, and Heather was fucking sick to the core of it.

It wasn't always like that, though.

Back when Abby was a little baby, Heather had been very caring about her. She used to hold her a lot and sing lullabies to her. She still remembered how baby Abby stared up at Heather with unblinking eyes, as if her big sister was God himself.

But when Abby grew up a little bit, trips to the hospital became commonplace. The spark in their parents' eyes was still there, albeit dimmer.

When Heather was old enough, they told her about Abby's condition and how she would never be able to live a normal life. Heather had still been too young to understand it fully back then, but the extent of Abby's condition became clear when the parents' entire attention shifted toward the younger sister.

Everything in their lives, including Heather's own life, was centered around Abby.

Want to go to the movies with friends? Too bad, Abby needs attention.

You turned off your phone for an hour? What if your sister needed you? You're grounded for a month.

You want to apply to a college? Fine, as long as it's a college in Witherton because your sister needs you here. Also, maybe you can get a medical degree that'll help you take care of Abby.

Ever since Abby arrived, Heather grew up always feeling like she was less important than Abby. For years, she tried to get her parents' attention, to make them proud, to make them acknowledge her. Like that one time she was chosen to give a speech in front of the whole school, and their family never showed up.

And then they died, and she never got to earn their love like she wanted to.

So when she saw Abby playing with her puzzle on the floor of the betting place, talking to herself, oblivious to everything, perky as if life went on normally, she wanted to slap her hard.

Abby looked up at Heather and said, "Sis, I need to pee."

"The bathroom's over there." Heather aloofly motioned to the door in the back.

"Can you go with me?" Abby asked.

"You're a big girl. You can go on your own."

Abby looked shocked. Heather was waiting for her to say something. *Go on. Test my fucking limits, you brat.*

"Okay." Abby stood and waltzed into the bathroom.

The thick tension in the air disappeared the moment Abby went through the door.

Heather exhaled a trembling breath into her hands. The anger that had taken hold of her with such intensity was gone, leaving Heather shaking from the emotions.

Pull yourself together, Heather.

She pulled out her phone to check for notifications. Nothing still. She tried to connect to a nearby wi-fi hotspot. No luck.

"Dammit," she said.

She needed a day in nature, alone, surrounded by nothing but wilderness. Just one day away from everything familiar so she could catch a break.

She realized that Abby had been gone for a few minutes. She already regretted being so brusque with Abby. Heather stood and walked into the bathroom. The interior split into the men's and women's bathrooms.

"Abby?" Heather called out as she entered the women's bathroom.

Abby stood in front of the stalls, facing away from Heather.

"Abby, what are you—" Heather froze a step shy of Abby.

She couldn't see her own face, but she imagined the color draining from it until it was pallid. Icy claws gripped the back of her neck and slithered down her spine.

A woman was seated against the far wall, her head slumped forward. Her legs were missing, mangled stumps where the knees should have been. The hair that fell over her face was sticky with blood and… something brown that smelled fetid. The same substance covered her torso and the floor, and Heather suppressed a reflexive gag that raced into her throat.

"Um… let's, uh…" Heather stammered. "Let's use the other bathroom."

"But that's the men's bathroom," Abby said.

"Now, Abby."

"But what about the girl?" Abby pointed.

"Abby…"

"Rah!" someone said.

The bulging eyes on Abby's face left no questions unanswered. When Heather followed Abby's gaze back to the legless woman, her head was no longer slumped. She was staring right at Heather with bloodshot eyes.

"She's one of the red-eyed people," Abby said.

She's still alive!

Something screamed inside Heather, bloating her chest to maximum tension. The woman's gaze was dull as if she'd been drugged. She must have been in shock because of her missing legs. How she was even still alive was a miracle.

The woman raised a hand and reached toward Abby.

"Fif… Fifty…" she said in a raspy voice.

Not drugged. That gaze was something entirely different, something Heather had never seen before. Her features were devoid of all human emotions, replaced by a primitive instinct—and whatever that instinct was, it commanded violence.

"Fifty!" the woman cawed.

"She's trying to tell us something!" Abby stepped forward.

"Stay away from her!" Heather jerked Abby back so feverishly that her little sister almost fell.

"Ow! Heather! Let me go!" Abby tried to free her hand.

"Wool. Wool. Wool…" the woman said before Heather realized that she was actually saying "wolves."

"Heather, you're hurting me!" Abby screamed.

"Abby! Calm down! Listen to me. Just listen to me!" Heather put her hands on Abby's cheeks and leaned closer to her. "Remember what I told you? None of this is real. It's just a trick to get you to expose yourself. It's just a trick. Just a trick."

Heather couldn't help repeating the sentence. She was in shock, and she felt sick, and her knees quivered, straining to keep the weight of her body upright. She needed to leave the bathroom immediately before she collapsed.

The woman's stiff fingers feebly clawed at the air as she muttered incoherent, throaty words.

"We're still playing the game. Okay? She saw us, which means we got some negative points. Now, we have to go before more of them see us, okay? Okay?"

Abby gave Heather a series of fervent nods. Heather pulled her out of the bathroom and closed the door tightly behind her. The woman kept flailing her arm in the air even as the door closed. Heather made sure to check the men's bathroom before letting Abby inside. It was dirty, but not with blood or corpses.

"I'll be waiting out here," Heather said and ushered Abby inside.

As Heather waited in front of the door, she could hear the woman in the bathroom uttering muffled, imperceptible words, one by one, with long pauses in-between, like spewing pieces of a puzzle that needed to be put together.

Those pieces wouldn't fit, though. Every word the woman spoke was a piece of an entirely different puzzle until an amalgamation of a picture was formed, incoherent, painted with shades of only two colors—red and brown. But among that jumbled information of her broken humanity, one intention would stand out. One instinct that shaped the existence of the red-eyed people.

The instinct to kill.

Boris Bacic

PIERCE

"Alpha, come in," the radio crackled.

Against the silence of the school's interior, it sounded loud enough to attract unwanted attention.

"This is Alpha," Reynolds said.

"What's your status?"

"We had to take a detour to lose the hostiles. Gonna make our way to the back entrance and proceed to the objective from there."

"Copy that. Watch yourselves. Out."

Most of the team members stood in a crude circle, facing each other. Only Pierce kept looking into the dark corridors that stretched on both ends, wondering what they'd find in that darkness.

"All right. Let's go," Reynolds said after looking both ways and choosing the right. "Lights."

Everyone turned on the torches on their rifles. Javelins of light pierced the air, casting some illumination but insufficient to disperse the darkness.

"Shit, not going that way," Lincoln said, pointing his light at the desks and chairs stacked down the hallway, a makeshift barricade blocking them from moving forward.

"The corridors go in a rectangle. We can go this way just the same." Pierce pointed in the other direction.

Reynolds nodded, and they started walking in the other direction.

Pierce didn't remember the school being this dark. When they walked past a window barred with planks nailed to the wall, he understood where the lack of daylight was coming from.

They moved quietly, each step of the boot muffled, but their heavy equipment still announced their presence, no matter how stealthy they tried to be. The corridor turned right and led past rows of classrooms.

Reynolds pointed to the closest door, and the team formed up for breaching and clearing. Pierce pressed his shoulder against the wall right next to the slightly ajar door and waited for Reynolds's command. When the captain nodded, Pierce pushed the door open and ran between the desks that seemed all too tiny compared to what they were in his memory.

The rest of the team swept inside, and then someone said, "Clear."

That meant Pierce could lower his weapon. If one of his team members shouted "clear," it meant they were sure it really was clear and safe to let his guard down—at least a little.

Lincoln closed the door behind them, which further increased the sense of thin safety. It didn't matter that the classroom, too, was engulfed in darkness. Pierce peeked through the cracks between the planks on the wall. The classroom overlooked part of the schoolyard. The rest of the view was obscured by imposing buildings that hadn't been there the last time Pierce was here.

"Ammo check," Reynolds said.

The sounds of mechanical clacking and clicking filled the classroom as they reloaded and counted their ammo. Pierce was good. He hadn't spent even half of his clip back outside.

"Catch your breaths, and then we're on our way," Reynolds said.

Pierce leaned on the windowsill and held his rifle by his side, scanning the classroom from left to right. This was Ms. Dunsky's classroom where she taught physics. Pierce often skipped her classes because he couldn't have cared less about the period. He wondered if she still worked at the school.

No, most likely retired, if not dead.

Pierce looked around, trying to remember the desk he used to sit at. His seat had been somewhere in the middle, but he couldn't remember which one. The desk had been rickety. Initials were carved into it, and the underside was bumpy with hardened bubblegum.

Then again, wasn't every high school desk like that?

"Hey," Shepherd leaned against the wall next to Pierce. "Why so nervous?"

"What? I'm not. Just waiting to get out of here."

"Liar. I could see how antsy you are from across the classroom. Something bothering you about this place?"

Pierce hadn't realized he was feeling uneasy until Shepherd called him out on it. Had Pierce been so obvious? Had Shepherd really noticed something, or was she bluffing?

He looked toward the other side of the classroom. Murphy was sitting on one of the desks, one foot dangling in the air, the other on the floor. Lincoln stood in front of him, saying something in a hushed voice. Meanwhile, Reynolds was standing near the door, his rifle gripped with alacrity.

Pierce reached behind his back, pulled out his water canteen, and took a sip. He nodded his head while allowing the liquid to slosh in his mouth for a moment before gulping. "I used to go to this high school."

"Bad memories tied to it?" Shepherd asked.

"Not the high school. This entire fucking town."

"You said you left Witherton at a young age, right?"

"Sixteen. After I shot my stepdad for beating me every night."

"You killed him?"

"Fuck, no. Although I wish I had. I was aiming for his leg, and I accidentally hit the knee."

Shepherd winced. Even hitting the knee on a table was painful as hell. Getting it blown off… that pain must have been out of this world.

The image of Gabriel writhing on the floor, holding his shattered knee, screaming in pain entered Pierce's mind. He could still feel the weight of the revolver in his teenage hands. It was as heavy as a brick. Squeezing the trigger proved to be an arduous task. The kickback was insane, and the gun almost ended up whacking Pierce in the face.

He remembered closing his eyes shut when the gun went off. When he opened them, his stepdad was on the ground.

His mother had been kneeling in front of Gabriel, her eyes bulging with terror. Pierce couldn't hear everything she was shouting because of his stepfather's screaming, but the words he did manage to make out followed him into his adulthood.

What did you do?!

What the fuck did you do?!

It was the last thing his mother would ever say to him. That terror-stricken face was the last one he'd ever see his mother make because, right after that—as soon as he saw her picking up the phone—he ran out of the house because he was afraid of dealing with the police. It only later occurred to him that she might have been trying to call an ambulance for Gabriel.

He didn't stop running until he was on the highway and a driver offered to give him a ride. It was a man in his twenties with dreadlocks and a mood too jovial. Loud rock music boomed from the car. Pierce accepted the offer and got into the car with the guy. The vehicle stank of weed and smoke, which explained the happy mood of the driver.

"Where you headed, dude?" he'd asked Pierce.

"I don't… I don't know. Drop me off wherever," Pierce had said atonally with a shrug.

"Sick!" the man replied and slammed the gas pedal, which made Pierce wonder if he'd even heard his response.

Hours later, he was in an unknown town he later learned was called Sweet Home. The irony didn't escape him.

He slept on the streets, shuddering every time a police cruiser would drive past him. He wondered if his stepfather was alive and if his mother was looking for him. He learned to survive the streets, but then he got caught stealing from a small shop one day. The owner was about to call the cops, but a man in a uniform who happened to be there offered to pay for the goods—and Pierce was sure there was some hush money there, too.

Pierce still remembered the uniformed man standing tall above him. He looked strong enough to fold Pierce like a balloon animal. Pierce had never felt as humiliated as he had at that moment, sitting on the stairs in front of the shop, dirty and in ragged clothes.

To his surprise, the man in the uniform smiled and offered a hand to Pierce. Pierce refused to accept it, unsure if it was some kind of a trap.

"Come with me. I might have something you'd be interested in," the man said in a deep voice.

That was how his military life began.

"Sorry. I shouldn't have pried," Shepherd said.

"You're good. It's in the past."

But even though he said that, he couldn't suppress the unease that tightened his chest.

Shepherd gave him a pat on the shoulder, something between a motherly and brotherly gesture.

"Time to go, Alpha," Reynolds said.

Everyone was up on their feet and ready to move. Maybe it was the gloomy atmosphere of the school getting to them. Maybe it was the homicidal infected that made them want to finish their mission more urgently.

Either way, no one objected to the captain's orders, least of all Pierce. The sooner they got out, the better.

Reynolds approached the door and gently opened it. The team converged at his side, and then—

A single, loud bang exploded in the classroom. Pierce's gun was already raised, just like everyone else's. They turned toward the window where the sound had come from.

The meager light that crept into the classroom was more abundant. Shining the light down, Pierce noticed one of the planks that stood over the window moments ago now on the floor. It was the same window Pierce had been leaning on, and he wondered if that had somehow caused the plank to topple.

A moment of suspenseful silence filled the classroom.

"Scared the hell out of me," Murphy said.

Reynolds shook his head then turned to face the entrance again.

That was when another sound came, giving the entire team pause once more.

Something loud crashed upstairs. And then came the sound of something scraping against the floor—chairs or desks possibly. Those sounds weren't accidental.

They were like a Morse code response to the sound caused by the fallen plank, to let Alpha Team know they were aware of their presence.

JAMES

"Parasite?" James echoed, still in shock from what had happened just before. "I don't understand. How do you know this?"

Angela sighed, the gesture of someone who had already explained this a thousand times and now had to do it for the thousand and first time. "You remember when I said that I work for Welco Labs?"

"Yeah? Wait... please, don't tell me you're actually a scientist who's worked on developing this parasite thing?"

Angela shook her head. "Please. That's insulting." The lopsided smile that crept onto her face told James she was being sarcastic. "No, I'm still a cleaner for Welco. But the guy who I told you put in a word for me? His name's Daniel. He and I had a thing for a while. That's actually why he put in a good word for me in the first place."

Angela looked away when she said that, clearly embarrassed.

"We still keep in touch as friends. He'd already told me about an experiment with a parasite they were conducting at the lab, but he couldn't share any details. Earlier today, he sent me a message telling me to get out of the city because things would get nasty."

"He knew?" Ricky asked.

"No clue. I'm assuming whatever they were experimenting on got out. I'm assuming that's what caused all of this. But that's all a wild guess."

"Why didn't you leave when you had the chance?" James asked.

"I tried to, but I couldn't. People were already panicking and rushing to reach the east exit. That caused heavy roadblocks. And fights. You had to be there to see how bad it was. People were killing each other just to cut in line before the person standing in front of them."

James needed a second to process this information. He was about to ask Angela why she hadn't told them about this earlier. He then realized that she probably would have once they were safely out of the town. The information was interesting, but not helpful to them in any way.

"Wait, you said that we all have it inside of us. What did you mean by that?" Ricky asked.

"Wish I could tell you." Angela sighed. "That's what Dan had told me months ago. When I asked him what kind of a parasite it was, he said it was a very common one and that most of us have it inside us."

James hung his head down, thinking. He didn't know anything about parasites. He knew that some bacteria existed that thrived inside the human body, but when ingested orally, they would wreak havoc on the organism. Maybe this was something similar.

"Look, we can sit around speculating all night long," Angela said. "Even if we get some answers, it won't help us get out. In fact, it'll put us in more danger. We need to reach that checkpoint."

"Now that we know it's a parasite, how do we even know they'll let us leave?" Ricky spread his arms quizzically.

"We still don't know what the military's orders are."

"Yeah! And that's exactly why we should be careful about throwing ourselves into the hands of armed men."

Angela stood up and turned to face Ricky. Ricky's hands had been on his hips, but they drooped when Angela stood. He seemed to shrink in front of her.

"Look, we can either take our shot with the checkpoint or sit and wait until someone decides to rescue the civilians. But that may take a while. And besides, you said that you heard they wanted to nuke the city, right?"

Ricky's lips pressed into a thin line. *Damn, she's right* was what that look said. Sure enough, the words followed a moment later.

"Okay, fine. We'll go for the checkpoint. But I'm keeping my distance."

"Suit yourself." Angela's head whipped toward James. "You coming?"

More than anything, James was just happy that his life wasn't over. Had this been a virus…

He didn't want to think in that direction. He was just glad that he got a second chance. He wasn't going to squander it. His eyes fell on Travis's lifeless body mere feet away from him.

"Sure as hell not staying here," he said as he stood up.

KRISTA

Something was wrong with Nelson.

Two days after Eric's departure, Krista entered Nelson's room to see him sitting upright at the edge of the bed. At first, she was exuberant because for him to be sitting meant that his fever was gone—or at least subsided enough for him to get out of bed.

She checked his forehead, and, sure enough, it was cool to the touch. Overnight, it had gone from hot to icy. She should have been glad, but that sudden change only made her more wracked with worry.

When Krista tried to talk to Nelson, though, he met her responses with a catatonic stare. She tried snapping her fingers in front of his face and asking him various questions, but he remained unresponsive.

After a while, he finally spoke, but it was a squeak of an imperceptible word. Krista had asked him to repeat what he said, but Nelson remained quiet.

The way he stared in one spot with a dead look worried Krista. Despite being devoid of all emotions, there was something in that look she couldn't put her finger on—something familiar that terrified her.

She brought him his favorite food—spaghetti—but he didn't even look at it. She left it on his nightstand and told him to eat it when he felt like it. Hours later, she went back to see the food intact and Nelson in the same position on his bed.

Krista figured it would have been better not to disturb him. For all she knew, he had changed positions in the past few hours while she was gone. Did she really believe that? She wanted to, and a mother's wish for her child to get better was strong enough to convince even the most stubborn minds to believe something that wasn't there.

For the rest of that day, Krista stared out the window, hoping to see movement outside, hoping for Eric to come back. She had been so lonely and scared since he left. Even if they didn't do anything to make Nelson better, just having him around soothed her nerves.

Alone, with Nelson's ever-changing condition keeping her on her toes and wondering whether her husband had already become another corpse in the street, she felt like she was losing her mind.

She tried to occupy herself by reading but found that she couldn't focus. The TV channels were blank, so she couldn't watch the news anymore, either. That made her feel as though the TV was getting back at her for turning it off days prior.

She tried playing Eric's Playstation, but she was so bad it only made her feel worse. Reading was too passive, and she got distracted easily.

Eventually, she went back to staring out the window. The neighborhood was too quiet, and as the hours passed, Krista started to convince herself that maybe it wouldn't be so dangerous to step outside. Maybe one of the neighbors had a working phone. Maybe they knew something about rescue or whatever the government was organizing.

In fact, staying locked up inside the house wouldn't do them any good.

She had lulled herself into the safety of those thoughts so deeply that she fully believed it was okay to step outside. She went to the door and reached for the lock. She could already imagine what fresh air would feel like on her face. It made her tremble with excitement.

But something interrupted her reverie. Something behind her. Not a sound but rather something that distinctly felt like a presence in the room. Krista turned around and pressed her lips tightly to stop herself from screaming at the figure that stood motionless.

Her hand was on her chest, and she could feel how wildly her heart was pumping against her ribcage.

"Jesus, Nelson. You scared me," she said with a nervous laugh.

Nelson stood in the middle of the foyer, staring up at Krista with a blank expression. He opened his mouth, and a single word escaped his mouth.

"What did you say?" Krista leaned closer to him.

"Toy," he repeated.

"Toy?" Krista asked to confirm whether that was what he had really said.

He didn't respond.

"What toy would you like?" she asked.

"Sleep," Nelson said, another clipped word.

"Baby, I don't understand. What are you saying?"

"Toy!" Nelson shouted in Krista's face so loudly that she reeled back in startlement.

Before she could respond to him, Nelson spun on the ball of his bare feet and ran back upstairs into his room, leaving Krista baffled and even more worried than before.

There was one thing that she somehow managed to neglect until then, and only by replaying the conversation with Nelson in her mind did she realize what it was.

The fact that his eyes were bloodshot.

HEATHER

Heather and Abby remained quiet while walking through the streets. Despite the area being empty, Abby refrained from asking questions as she usually did. Either she could sense Heather's frustration and knew it was a bad time to get on her nerves, or she was too tired.

It had been a long day. The sun was starting to set, and the sisters had barely made any progress. The detours they had to take only seemed to lead them farther away from the goal. Heather knew they'd be able to skirt the red-eyed people for only so long. To reach the military checkpoint, they would probably need to go through the throng that occupied the streets.

It wasn't a question of whether the way to the checkpoint would be clear. It was a question of how many of them they'd encounter along the way.

Heather had thought they'd done a good job sneaking around them all day long, but the lack of progress spoke for itself. It was too late to worry about it at the moment because, with the day ending, the sisters had to find shelter.

The veil of night might have provided cover for them, but they'd been walking way too much, and they needed to be well-rested in order to survive.

"I'm hungry, Sis. Can we eat?" Abby said at one point, her voice devoid of tonality.

"You already asked me that, and I already told you we need to find a safe place before we can eat," Heather said, her nerves frayed with irritation.

"But where is the safe place?"

Heather chose to ignore that question because she found no point in answering it. Giving Abby an answer would only incite more questions. It was a bottomless hole.

"When is the game going to end? I wanna see the reward," Abby said.

"It's not an easy game. You think they'd just serve the reward on a silver platter? You have to work for it. For once in your life."

Abby didn't get the remark, of course.

"Is it going to finish today?"

"No."

"Then when?"

"When I... when I say so." She wanted to say *when I fucking say so* but avoided swearing in front of Abby, no matter how much she annoyed her.

"I don't want to play anymore," Abby said.

"Well, too bad. We started it, and we left the apartment for it, and there's no way to go back without walking for hours. So if you wanna wuss out and run home, be my guest. Find your own way back."

Abby hung her head down and continued walking.

Good. That's what I thought.

How did their parents ever make it through so many years with Abby? She was insufferable.

Hell, how had Heather made it so long with her? She was starting to consider she was at her wit's end with her little sister. If she had more money, she would have put her in one of those care centers where children with special needs lived.

She saw an ad for it once. It was like a school but also provided housing to the children. The hefty pricing had made Heather exit the website immediately. Not that she'd be able to afford it anyway with waitressing, but she had been curious about it.

Abby said nothing more for the duration of the walk. Heather knew she'd hurt her little sister's feelings, but she didn't care. In fact, it felt good to do so. It felt like she was finally getting the justice she deserved, even if it was a tiny fragment.

And unlike before, their parents weren't there to reprimand Heather for mistreating her sister.

After a few more minutes of walking, they found a restaurant where they could stay for the night. It bothered Heather beyond words to have to stay overnight in an unfamiliar place, the checkpoint still so far from their sight. She would have made it had she gone on her own because she would have taken the risk of sneaking directly past the red-eyed people.

With her sister at her side, though, she had to go for the safest possible route she could find because she didn't know if Abby would gasp or scream or do something else to attract the red-eyed people. If that happened, it would be game over. Heather stood no chance against them, especially if there were more of them.

And there were always more of them.

Heather closed and locked the door behind her. The interior of the restaurant seemed pretty much intact, save for a few tables that still had plates of unfinished food on them.

"Guess we're staying here for the night," Heather said, more to herself than to Abby.

"Can I get chicken nuggets?" Abby asked.

"No."

"Why?"

"Because the restaurant isn't open."

"But we're inside. That means it works, right?"

"Abby…" Heather started, poised for another mean remark. "Why don't you find a table where you can sit? Play your puzzle while I get us some food."

"Okay."

Abby took off her school bag and hopped on a chair while Heather made her way down toward the kitchen. She found leftover foods scattered on the countertops. One untouched pizza sat on a platter. It would have made for a perfect dinner had flies not been buzzing around it, and it looked shriveled.

Must have been sitting out for days.

Heather looked in the fridge. Most of the ingredients were raw, but she did find some chicken nuggets and cakes. She put the nuggets in the microwave and found some utensils for the slices of cake.

While she waited for the nuggets, it crossed her mind that she was stealing food from the restaurant. She quickly dismissed that thought, justifying that the craziness in Witherton made people abandon their homes and businesses, which meant it was free for looting.

She wondered how Wonder Meal Diner was doing and if it was still open. She was still angry at Dwayne for being so unreasonable about her not showing up to work.

It gave her petty satisfaction to know that he was probably forced to close his precious diner. She could just imagine him pacing back and forth, fuming about the government not helping small businesses, as he always did.

Good.

Heather didn't know why she even took his crap for such low pay. The tiny voice inside the restaurant playing with the puzzle reminded her why.

The microwave dinged, indicating that the chicken nuggets were done. She put them on two separate plates, which she carried back to the guest area. When she arrived at the table where Abby had been sitting, all she found were the messily scattered pieces of the puzzle.

Abby was not there.

A jolt of panic speared Heather's abdomen until she looked toward the entrance. Abby stood in front of the closed door, staring at the street outside. Heather placed the plates on the table and strode over to Abby, ignoring the dread that constricted her throat.

"Abby, what are you doing?" she asked.

Abby was frozen, exactly as she'd been in the bathroom where they found that woman, and that was what caused Heather to feel such a growing sense of fear.

"Abby," she called out to her again.

A shadow washed past the restaurant, just on the other side of the door. Heather snapped at the door, but it was already gone. The unease inside her was slowly reaching the border of panic.

"Red-eyed people," Abby said, her eyes plastered to the street outside.

Those words didn't help one bit. If anything, they made Heather feel like the danger was not only outside but in the restaurant with her.

As if Abby's sentence had somehow conjured a summoning spell, more figures appeared in the streets. One walked past the restaurant, then two in the opposite direction, then one more that stopped in the middle of the street where he stared up at the sky in a catatonic state.

"Move away from the window, Abby," Heather said.

"Why are they acting like that?" Abby asked.

"I… I don't know."

"Are they sick?"

"What makes you think they're sick?"

"Because I once saw a movie about sick people who had to go to hospitals. They were acting the same way as them."

She was talking about a mental institution. Come to think of it, the red-eyed people *did* behave like mentally ill patients. Sure, not all patients with mental problems exhibited such violent behavior, but what if this whole thing was a disease that spread by making people crazy?

But then, why weren't Abby and Heather like them?

The person who stared at the sky occasionally spasmed as if tasered just for a brief moment. Other red-eyed people walked past him, ignoring him. They walked strangely, stomping their feet, raising their knees high, slouching while their arms dangled by their sides… by all accounts, it looked as if they were losing motor capabilities in certain parts of their bodies.

Heather and Abby had been lucky to get inside a safe place before they were spotted. If they stayed out on the street for just a few more minutes…

"Why do we have to hide from them?" Abby asked.

"Because they want to hurt us," Heather said.

"Why? How do you know? Maybe they're just playing the game like us."

"Maybe," Heather said mostly to dismiss Abby's incessant questions.

"So, can we go talk to them?"

Heather opened her mouth to say no, but a thought interrupted her. She imagined Abby going out there to try to talk to the red-eyed people. They would not listen, of course. They understood only one language.

What would happen next was pretty clear. Heather had seen enough corpses today to last her for a lifetime to know the ending of an interaction with the red-eyed people would not be pretty.

It would be so easy to get rid of Abby. Heather fantasized about it many times in the past, but that was all it was—a fantasy. Yet, with the world going to hell, it didn't have to be only that anymore. It could become reality, and Heather would get out of it, free of consequences.

No more stupid questions, no more limitations. She'd be free. *Free.* To live her life as she always imagined it. The thought almost caused her to salivate.

All she had to do was say "yes" to Abby and then watch as she went out that door into her doom.

Heather wondered how quickly Abby would get killed. Would it be painful for her? Would she even have time to scream? Visits to the doctor were sometimes painful, but that didn't mean they were bad. Right?

This wouldn't be just for Heather's good. It would be for Abby's as well. What kind of a life could she possibly lead? She'd require constant care. Was that even a life worth living?

"Sure. You can go talk to them," Heather said.

Abby looked up at Heather with sparkling eyes. "Really?"

Her smile stretched from ear to ear.

"Yeah. I'll unlock the door for you."

Heather pinched the lock, her heart racing in her chest. She gently twisted it then waited to see if any of the red-eyed people would react to the click. They remained oblivious. Holding her breath, Heather stepped back and said, "There. You're good to go."

Abby's grin refused to abate. She put her hands together, visibly excited as she looked at Heather.

"Thanks. You're the best, Sis."

For a split second, Heather swore she could see a younger Abby standing in front of her, the little baby that had been brought from the hospital, beautiful in her innocence, staring up at Heather as she held her with eyes full of affection.

A lump formed in Heather's throat.

You're the best, Sis.

Something Abby said for the most trivial things, like when Heather made her cereal, tied her shoelaces, helped her with homework, let her play with the puzzle, or allowed her to stay up five minutes past her bedtime.

It wasn't just to express her unending love and gratitude. Her communication skills were limited, but that one sentence said a million things she'd never be able to express verbally. It showed that Abby understood Heather's sacrifices and that she didn't take them for granted, and that she loved and admired her so much for being such a selfless big sister.

All the hate and resentment toward Abby disappeared as quickly as air disappeared from a balloon. Warmth and love and care, and, most of all, *need* replaced those malicious emotions. Abby wasn't just some patient that Heather took care of. She was her sister.

And then, the crushing weight of realization hit Heather. She had just tricked Abby into sending her to her death.

"Abby, wait!" Heather broke into a dash after her.

Abby was already through the door. The red-eyed man that had been staring at the sky looked down at the commotion. His slack features contorted into a hateful grimace. He looked so much like the woman from the bathroom.

Heather grabbed her by the arm and pulled her back inside. She closed the door just in time to hear a blood-curdling scream come from the street.

"Ow!" Abby said at the tug.

There was no time to waste. Heather sprinted into the kitchen, pulling Abby's hand behind her. She ignored Abby's complaints because she was too busy hearing the door burst open, and then a monstrous growl tore through the restaurant's interior.

They ran inside the kitchen. Heather closed the door then darted her eyes around the room for a hiding spot. The first and only thing that her eyes fell on was the counter. She pulled Abby and herself under it just when the door burst open loudly.

She held her sister tightly under the table, shaking violently. Abby, on the other hand, seemed completely calm. Their eyes met. Heather could see that Abby had questions, so she quickly raised a finger to her mouth. Abby remembered what that gesture meant because she pressed her lips together tightly.

Silence enveloped the kitchen, but only briefly.

Growling resounded from the door, followed by shuffling footsteps. Distant screams encroached on the restaurant. Heather could hear more of them coming inside, attracted by the one who had screeched first.

A pair of feet appeared in front of the table—tattered shoes smeared with blood and dirt, above them, jeans, the bottom of which was soaked in mud. With the person came the unmistakable odor of death.

Heather clamped a hand over her mouth to stop herself from screaming. Tears blurred her vision and trickled down her cheeks as she stared, waiting for a bloodied head to appear under the table with a wide grin.

Found you.

Should she wait and hope for the best? Or strike while she still had the element of surprise? She felt like she was going crazy.

Then a ray of calmness found itself into her in the form of a squeeze of her hand. Heather looked toward Abby, who was still tight-lipped, giving Heather a certain look. Was it supposed to be a look of reassurance? Was Abby even capable of doing that, or was it just Heather's panicked mind grasping at straws?

The feet shuffled back the way they came, one foot dragged behind the other.

Heather allowed the hand to let go of her mouth, and she exhaled a tentative, quivering breath. More emboldened, she peeked out toward the spot where the red-eyed person had disappeared. He was moving away from them, back into the restaurant.

Heather retreated under the table then leaned closer to Abby and whispered, "We have to sneak out back. But we have to be very, very quiet. Okay?"

Abby nodded.

Heather peeked out once more. The red-eyed person was still in the kitchen, in front of the door, staring up at the ceiling just as he had stared at the sky outside. After a long minute, it became apparent he wasn't planning on moving, so Heather and Abby had to go.

Getting on all fours, Heather quietly crawled out, holding her breath and listening to the raspy breathing at the door. Once she was out, she peeked above the counter.

The red-eyed man turned his head to the left. Heather's heart leaped into her throat. The red-eyed man faced forward again, continuing to stare at the ceiling.

Heather motioned for Abby to follow her. Her little sister crawled out in a similar fashion. The two of them crawled around the counter toward the backdoor. Something loudly clattered in the kitchen, causing Heather to freeze.

She expected to hear screaming and a stampede of footsteps. Instead of that, a new sound entered the kitchen. Footsteps were followed by the high-pitched and repetitive clearing of a throat. The noise traveled down the length of the other side of the counter.

Another loud clatter and the circular reverberation of what might have been pots spinning on the ground as they lost momentum. Something shattered on the floor. Once that noise receded, the phlegmatic clearing of the throat resumed.

Heather raised her head then immediately brought it back down. In the moment that she looked up, she saw a woman, not dissimilar to the one they'd seen in the bathroom: dirty, haggard, sticky with blood.

The footsteps trailed back toward the door. The pot that had been knocked down clanged again, probably kicked by the woman. Heather raised her head once more. Both red-eyed people in the kitchen were facing away from them.

This was their chance to get away.

Heather crawled forward, and once she was in front of the door, she got up into a kneeling position and opened the door. She waved Abby over to get through. Abby crawled through the gap. Heather followed her.

Once they were outside, they were up on their feet and running away from the restaurant as fast as their legs could carry them.

DANIEL

Richard bucked against the straps that held him bound to the examination table. The leather dug into his wrists, ankles, and neck, leaving deep abrasions that didn't seem to bother him. His teeth clacked with each bite of the air as he tried to reach Daniel in vain. His fingers contracted and relaxed intermittently as he supinated his hands in an attempt to break them free.

"Escape!" Richard shouted. "No more! Amino acids!"

He'd been speaking gibberish ever since he came to. Daniel had seen similar behavior with the other infected—screaming words that seemed like they were a missing piece of a puzzle.

Daniel stood above his former colleague, staring at him in both fascination and disgust. How had this happened to Richard so fast? Just a few hours ago, he had looked okay. Or had he?

Even down at the reception, he had been pale and sweating a lot. And then he had said he was feeling unwell. A fever, perhaps?

If that was the case, then maybe Daniel's initial assumption had been right—they were dealing with a virus or bacteria.

"Lie still, Richard. I need to draw your blood," Daniel said as he prepared the syringe and needle.

"Lock the door! Jacket!" Spittle flew out of Richard's mouth.

Richard, of course, continued thrashing against his restraints, refusing to comply. The straps that held him down did most of the work for Daniel. All he needed to do was pin his arm to the table for stability as he inserted the needle in Richard's arm.

Richard's lurching bent the needle in his arm and made it difficult for Daniel to focus, but eventually, he managed to get a sample.

"There. That wasn't so bad, right?" He grinned.

A harsh way to joke? Perhaps. But humor was Daniel's way of dealing with things. That and work.

If he didn't do that, he'd go down the rabbit hole of speculating whether he or the other two surviving staff members in the building were infected, how long it would take them to become like Richard, whether the company would rescue them or deem them too much of a threat to keep them alive, and so on.

So yeah, working and cracking jokes was a healthy and inexpensive substitute for therapy.

Daniel labeled the test tube with the blood as RICH BLOOD and slid it into the vacant slot on the rack. He needed to test the blood, but first, coffee. It was late afternoon, and he'd been on his feet all day long. He needed the brown liquid that would fuel him late into the night.

Maybe a meal, too, he thought to himself when he remembered he hadn't eaten anything since lunch, and the cardio that he wasn't used to had drained him.

The kitchen always had donuts, bagels, pretzels, and other snacks that employees of Welco Labs could nab during break.

"You wait right here, Richard," Daniel said as he yanked the rubber gloves off and tossed them on the floor—no need to worry about keeping the place tidy with all the blood and scattered tools on the floor.

He leisurely walked past a hissing Richard then stopped and turned his head toward him. "I'll try to find a cure for you, buddy. I promise."

He didn't believe he'd find it.

***

When Daniel entered the kitchen, Melissa was there, seated behind one of the tables, her hands cradling the plastic cup from which steam billowed. Her head had been slumping toward the cup when Daniel stepped inside, and then she looked up at him.

"Oh, hey." She brushed her hair behind her ear.

"Hi." Daniel offered a smile.

The smell of coffee pleasantly invaded his nostrils, making him crave it even more.

"Is he..." Melissa started.

"Oh, he's strapped down. I drew his blood, and I'm going to run some tests right after I've had some coffee."

Melissa stared at Daniel dumbfounded. Daniel realized too late that his response sounded like he was making casual small talk on a normal working day, which this wasn't.

"How can you be so calm about all of this, Dan?" she asked.

Daniel approached the coffee machine and began working it. "Someone has to keep a cool head in this situation." Melissa looked offended. "I didn't mean... you know what? Forget it."

His patience for dealing with bullshit was a lot thinner today. He made coffee then leaned his rear on the counter as he raised the cup to his mouth, savoring the smell before taking a sip.

"Do you..." Melissa cleared her throat. "Do you need help at the lab?"

"No." Daniel shook his head and took another sip. "Did Skinner remove Sharpe from the hallway?"

"Yes. He dragged him into one of the offices."

"Did he lock the door?"

Melissa snapped her head up. Everything about her had been lethargic except that motion.

"I don't know," she said. "Should he?"

"Yes."

"Why?"

Because I don't know if this is a zombie virus or something that reanimates people, and we don't want Sharpe getting the drop on us like Richard.

"It's probably safer," Daniel said instead.

"Okay. Um, I'll tell him."

"Cool. Did you manage to get in touch with your husband?"

The only reason why he'd asked that was because he couldn't stand the awkward funeral-like silence in the kitchen.

Melissa shook her head. "I tried calling and texting, but he hasn't responded. I really hope he's okay."

Daniel took another sip of coffee. He let the liquid slosh around in his mouth before gulping, to avoid responding to Melissa.

The donuts he'd been craving were no longer on his mind. He just wanted out of the kitchen as soon as possible so he could go back to work. Richard's vicious growling was preferrable to Melissa's moping.

Still, he couldn't suppress the pang of pity that he felt toward her as he watched her sitting in front of her cup, biting her lip and tapping her foot on the floor. A million thoughts must have raced through her head; the same ones that would have raced through his head had he chosen not to keep himself occupied.

"I should get back to work," he finally said, taking the cup with him.

"Dan?" Melissa called out to him softly when he reached the door.

He turned to face her, dreading her next sentence, question, suggestion, or whatever she had to say.

"About what happened earlier," she said.

"What exactly are you referring to?"

"When I yelled at Skinner to shoot Richard, I shouldn't have done that."

"Oh?" Daniel cocked an eyebrow.

"I was scared, but it was irrational of me to ask Skinner to shoot one of our own. Richard is still alive, and when rescue comes, they might be able to help save him."

"Richard is not one of our own. He's a coworker who happened to find himself in the same mess as us."

Daniel could tell by Melissa's facial expression that she didn't approve of his response but said nothing about it.

"Look, if it makes you feel any better, it was probably the right call, trying to convince Skinner to kill Richard."

"It was?" Melissa seemed surprised by Daniel's indirect compliment.

"If it had been me in Richard's shoes... Hell, if I do go crazy like him, I'd want you guys to kill me."

"I... I don't think I'd be able to do that." Melissa crossed her arms, and her shoulders tensed up.

"You didn't seem to have a problem with that when it was Richard."

"Yes, but I know you better than I knew Richard."

It didn't go over Daniel's head that Melissa used the past tense when referring to Richard—as if he was already dead.

"So, is that where we're drawing lines, now? We're perfectly fine killing someone infected unless it's friends and family?" Daniel asked.

"No, that's not what I..."

"I'd be safe because you know me better than Richard?"

"No, I mean, killing someone you know would be harder, but... I didn't..." Melissa was blushing, and Daniel took great amusement from her getting worked up so much, but not in a sadistic kind of way. He just found it cute.

"Relax, Melissa." He grinned. "I was just joking."

"Oh. Of course. I probably should have realized it." Melissa's nostrils dilated and narrowed, and she sounded like she was out of breath. She cleared her throat, scanned the room as if looking for a lost item, and said, "I'm going to see what Skinner is up to."

"Sure. If you get bored later, you can stop by the lab."

"I thought you said you didn't need help."

"I don't, but a second opinion is often very helpful."

"Okay. I might do that."

Daniel turned to leave at last before craning his neck to face Melissa once more. "Oh, but heads up, the lab is full of blood, and Richard is kind of restless, so if that bothers you..."

He made a grimace without finishing his sentence and then returned to the lab, savoring the look of terror on Melissa's face.

***

Even hours later, Richard refused to calm down. Where he got so much strength from baffled Daniel. The infection might have rerouted non-essential bodily functions to give the host more physical strength.

Would that even be possible?

After everything I've seen today? Yes, absolutely.

Daniel performed various tests on Richard, but he couldn't find anything that would indicate why he had gone crazy. He even attached an EEG to him to test his brain activity but received no conclusive answer.

The host was still alive, he at least knew that much. It wasn't a walking corpse whose motor functions were controlled by the infection. But something was going on there. Some of the functions of the brain had been minimized or even completely shut off while others went wild.

"I don't understand, Richard." Daniel spread his arms and shook his head. "What is happening to you?"

Richard growled and hissed and tore at his restraints. His eyes had turned more red since he was first tied to the exam table. The abrasions on his skin were bloody. It wouldn't be long before he scraped the flesh away to the bone.

Daniel had thought about sedating Richard, but what good would it do? As soon as he woke up, he would continue fighting, and Daniel couldn't keep him sedated at all times.

"I'm not giving up on you yet. There are still some tests we can perform. Something has gotta show up, Rich."

"I-is is everything okay?" Melissa stood at the door, peeking inside, her gaze curiously flitting toward Richard.

"Yes. You can come in. It's safe."

That was the only reason why she had come, Daniel assumed.

Melissa scanned the messy laboratory as if trying to decide whether it was safe to step in. She crossed the threshold with one giant step, and then every subsequent one came easier. She wrapped herself in her lab coat, probably worried she'd get blood on her clothes.

She stopped a few feet from the exam table and looked down at Richard with her upper lip raised in disgust. Richard jerked his head from Daniel to Melissa where he continued snapping at the air, even though she stood at a safe distance.

"Did you find out anything?" she asked.

"Nothing yet. But I still have some more tests to run. And a few theories."

"Like what?"

"This virus is something new. Something that's still learning how to use its hosts."

Melissa nodded. "It doesn't spread effectively. Patients of rabies develop hydrophobia in order to salivate more and, therefore, spread with more ease. We haven't seen any unique pattern of spreading here."

Daniel's lips contorted into a smile. It would seem that Melissa had entered her work mood just like Daniel. "That's an excellent observation. But there are other factors we haven't taken into consideration. Like whether the virus is airborne or whether it even is a virus. It could be anything, for all we know."

"What do you suppose it is?"

"What do *you* think it is?"

Melissa crossed her arms and looked down at Richard, a pensive look on her face. "People went crazy without any cause or indication. There wasn't an increased number of patients at the hospital just before the outbreak. Nothing to tell us it all started recently from a *patient zero* who had spread the infection."

"Precisely." Daniel nodded. "So, what does that tell us?"

Melissa inflated her chest with an inhale. "It tells us it's something we've had in us the entire time. Only now, it's mutated."

Boris Bacic

PIERCE

"What was that just now?" Shepherd asked.

She and Pierce were staring at the ceiling as if x-ray vision would help them see what lay above them.

"No idea," Reynolds said. "The building's probably infested with infected, and they might be shuffling around. Or maybe the noise we made caught the attention of something it wasn't supposed to. Either way, we'd best be careful."

They quietly exited the classroom and proceeded down the hall toward the back exit. It felt surreal seeing the school so quiet. Hearing bells ringing and the voices of teenagers chirping as they buzzed from one class to another had become so normal that silence made caution slither into Pierce's limbs.

A splash under Pierce's foot caused him to look down. His flashlight illuminated a glistening puddle of blood.

Still fresh. Someone died here recently.

Most classrooms were closed. Holes adorned some of them as if something punched a hole through the wood. Witherton South High never was known for its investment in quality renovations. In fact, during Pierce's time as a high schooler, the principal had been exposed as having used the school funds for his private jacuzzi. He resigned when faced with threats of pressed charges.

They walked past the stairs leading to the second floor. Reynolds, who had been at the front of the group, raised a hand. Everyone stopped. That was when Pierce heard it.

Steady creaking that went back and forth like an ambulance siren. It was coming from a nearby classroom.

Reynolds walked up to the door, squeezed the knob, and gently twisted it. The knob produced an *eee-eee* creak. Reynolds pushed the door open. It, too, squealed way too loudly against the contrast of the silence. Once it stopped, the creaking from before became more audible.

Eee-ooo-eee-ooo, the sound went.

Reynolds pointed his rifle and took one step inside the classroom, the other foot remaining out in the hallway. He retreated, turned to face the team, and raised a finger to his mouth, before tip-toeing down the hallway.

Pierce was dying of curiosity. What the hell was in there? An entire classroom full of infected kids? Something worse? He couldn't imagine what could possibly be worse than that.

Eee-ooo-eee-ooo, the sound in the classroom had turned irregular, often growing in pitch and volume and then going almost completely silent.

One by one, the squad members in front of Pierce sneaked in Reynolds's footsteps. When it was Pierce's turn, he slowed down when passing next to the classroom. It wasn't just the creaking that he heard anymore. Soft gasps accompanied the squeaks in tandem.

A boy sat at a desk, rocking back and forth in his chair. He was leaning on his elbows, his hands grasping clumps of his bushy hair so hard it looked like he was about to rip them out. Around him, the other desks had been trashed and overturned. Bodies littered the floor. Pierce was grateful he couldn't see their faces.

Eee-ooo-eee-ooo, the sound continued more mildly, as if the teenager sensed someone was watching him. Gasps were punctuated with sobs.

Pierce couldn't stand the sound. He leaned forward, took the doorknob into his hand, and gently pulled the door closed as far as he could without causing the lock to click in place. The creaking and gasping grew muffled. They disappeared entirely when he caught up to his team.

They ran into another open classroom before reaching the end of the hallway, but this one was empty save for a hairy, disembodied arm with a watch still attached to the wrist. They turned where the corridor led them and reached the backdoor.

"Shit," Reynolds said under his breath.

Pierce didn't need to ask what the bad news was. Tables and chairs were stacked along the passage like a house of cards. Pierce could see the exit just beyond the barricade, a door barred with a single metal pipe.

"Looks like we're not going out this way," Reynolds whispered and let out a frustrated sigh.

"We can use the stairs back the way we came." Pierce hooked a thumb behind him.

"What have you got in mind?" the captain asked.

"There are two sets of stairs. One on this side of the hallway and another across. Since the corridors of Witherton South High wind in a rectangle, we can go up to the second floor, circle to the other side, and then down the other set of stairs. It'll lead us right to the exit."

"Sounds good. Stick close, everyone," Reynolds said.

The creaking noise from the classroom was gone by the time they walked past it. Pierce glanced inside to see the desk previously occupied by the rocking student empty. He tried not to think about where he had gone. The sooner they got out of the school, the better.

Lincoln took point as they climbed the stairs, one step at a time. The beams of their torches were annoyingly narrow, insufficient to grant the illumination the team so desperately needed. Furthermore, using torches made Pierce feel vulnerable. They were broadcasting their position to anyone who could see their lights.

Before they reached the top of the stairwell, another loud crash came from somewhere close by, similar to the one they'd heard back at the classroom. Then, something heavy was getting dragged across the floor. It sounded like it was coming from just around the corner and slowly receding with each drag.

Lincoln, who was closest to the top of the stairs, jumped out into the hallway and pointed his rifle at the source of the sound. He gave the signal to the rest of the team to follow him.

The second floor was just as dark as the first one but not as empty. As soon as Pierce turned right, a face stared up at him from the floor. He resisted the urge to slide his finger across the trigger, and it turned out to be a good thing.

The face that gawked at him belonged to a dead body. Male, in his late twenties, maybe. A new teacher at Witherton South High, perhaps? A huge chunk of his throat was missing, semicircular ridges around the wound of his neck like the ones teeth left when a bite was taken out of food.

"You recognize him?" Shepherd whispered.

"No. He's too young. Probably started teaching here recently," Pierce said.

Staring down at those glassy eyes, he couldn't help but wonder who the dead guy was and how his last moments had unfolded.

Had he been proud to have landed a job as a teacher in Witherton's high school, or had he accepted it because there were no other opportunities for him? Whatever plans he'd had for the future were snuffed out by the outbreak that no one saw coming.

"Go on. I got your back," Pierce said to Shepherd as he took the rear of the group.

More bodies lay in the hallway, adults and teenagers alike, a lot of them badly mutilated. Alpha's pace significantly slowed down as they prudently made their way around the bodies, stepping over limbs and heads and torsos.

Pierce was too focused on watching his team's backs to look down at the faces. It was better that way, anyway. He was afraid of seeing some of those dead eyes opening and staring up at him accusingly—familiar faces of his former classmates forever stuck at the age they were when Pierce left Witherton, ready to pull him back into the depths of hell he'd lived through in his childhood.

He hadn't felt so restless around dead bodies since his first mission with the unit.

Coming to Witherton was a bad idea. They should have found someone else. He should have told HQ about his history with Witherton.

A patter of rapid footsteps came from behind Pierce. He whirled around fast, his rifle trained ahead of him. A silhouette disappeared around the corner of the hallway where the footsteps immediately stopped.

Not faded. Stopped.

Whoever ran behind that corner was standing there, right near the edge, waiting for Pierce's light to swivel away. Pierce lowered the barrel of his rifle but continued staring at the corner where he'd seen the shape disappear.

Nothing.

He raised the rifle again, but all his cone revealed was an empty hallway and the dead teacher from before.

"Pierce!" Shepherd hissed.

The others were already down the hall, disappearing one by one around the corner where the corridor turned. Pierce gave Shepherd a curt nod, looked at the spot where he'd seen the silhouette running, then caught up to his team. He peeked behind once more before turning the corner just to make sure nothing would sneak up on him.

A message was scrawled on the wall on this side of the corridor.

WE'RE ALL DEAD, it said in crude, red letters like a mimicry straight out of a horror video game.

One of the classrooms was filled with students who stood motionless in front of their desks as if paying respects to the national anthem that would never end. Similar to the classroom where they encountered the rocking student, Alpha Team walked past the infected students without arousing suspicion.

They made another turn and then another. They just needed to reach the stairs, and they'd be out of this claustrophobia-inducing place.

Soft clicking was coming from somewhere. It might have been a completely normal sound like pipes or something similar, but in a situation like this one, nothing was normal or harmless. Still, only Pierce seemed to be concerned by it as the rest of the team plodded forward, ignoring the noise.

The sound grew in volume as Pierce walked forward, and it was coming from a nearby classroom.

"You guys hear that?" Pierce asked, but his voice betrayed him; came out as a ghost of a question.

He stopped and hung his head down to focus on the sound. The others continued walking, unaware that Pierce had fallen behind.

The sound was as cryptic as the one the rocking student made on the floor below, and not being able to place it bothered Pierce. He squeezed his eyes shut to eliminate the visual distractions and focused on the incessant noise.

No longer clicking, the sound had transmogrified into soft, muffled banging. And then a voice. Two words startled Pierce enough to open his eyes and look around, wondering if he'd imagined everything.

"Help me."

The rest of Alpha's squad was nearing the stairs. Pierce hesitated. Even after years and years of training to react fast to unpredictable scenarios, he found himself hesitating for the first time in forever. Then again, this wasn't a typical scenario. How many soldiers and police officers had died during this outbreak because they couldn't pull the trigger when an infected child or pregnant woman ran after them or because they underestimated the infected and got swarmed, or became infected themselves?

"Help me," as if to confirm Pierce's suspicions, the voice said again.

It belonged to a woman.

"Hey," Pierce called out to his team, but again, no one responded.

He looked toward the classroom where the banging persisted. He would be quick. Go in, help the woman if she needed it, and then catch up with his team.

He opened the classroom and stepped inside.

"Help me," the voice said.

It was still muffled. The banging turned into clinking.

Pierce looked around the classroom. His torch illuminated a chained and padlocked storage closet at the back of the classroom. The chains rattled with each bang.

"Hold on," Pierce said, his voice still a murmur.

He walked to the other side of the classroom and stopped in front of the door. Blood smeared the door handle and the edge of the frame. The key was still in the padlock. One turn and the chains would drop, releasing the person inside.

"What happened to you? Who locked you in there?" Pierce asked.

"Help me," the woman repeated, the banging never ceasing.

She must have been in shock. Maybe delirious from dehydration and starvation, depending on how long she'd been stuck in there.

"Hang on. I'll get you out of there," Pierce said.

He reached for the key when the woman spoke again. "Help me."

Pierce would have grabbed and turned the key without a second thought had the woman not repeated that sentence again. That caused his hand to freeze mid-air, hovering above the key.

Help me.

It wasn't what the woman had said but the way she'd said it. Always the same intonation, the same sigh-like *help* and clipped *me.*

The chains continued rattling. A trickle of sweat tickled Pierce's temple. Was his assumption right that the person inside was infected? Was that why she was locked up?

But she was speaking. Could infected speak? What if it was a person who needed help? If Pierce left her here, she would surely die. If he opened the door, she'd at least have a chance to survive.

"Help me," the woman said.

Pierce had already made up his mind. He'd open the door. If the person inside turned out to be a hostile, he'd take her down with his combat knife. He was confident in his abilities to do that.

His hand inched toward the key. The chains clanged with more intensity the closer Pierce's fingertips got. The second his forefinger and thumb pinched the key, the disturbance stopped.

No more shaking, no more pleading for help. Pierce licked his dry lips. He turned the key—

A hand fell on his shoulder.

Pierce whipped around with a stifled gasp, batting the hand away.

"Don't," Shepherd said.

Pierce felt like he'd just sobered up after drinking one too many. He blinked at Shepherd then looked back at the chains holding the storage closet locked.

"We're waiting for you. Come on," Shepherd stepped aside to make way for Pierce.

Pierce's gaze intermittently bounced from Shepherd to the padlock. He then nodded, refusing to look at Shepherd any longer out of shame, and left for the classroom's exit.

By the time they were out, the chains were rattling again, and the woman's repetitive "help me" had turned into growling.

When Pierce and Shephard reached the stairs, the others were waiting for them. Reynolds gave Pierce an admonishing look, but rather than say anything, he started descending the stairs.

When they regrouped at the bottom of the stairs, Reynolds said, "Everybody, stay close. I don't want anyone falling behi—"

His sentence was cut off when the light from his gun illuminated a figure down the hall.

"Fuck," Pierce heard Murphy say next to him through clenched teeth.

Pierce needed a moment to comprehend what he was seeing because it looked so absurd he half-believed this place was fucking with his head.

Not just one figure. A whole bunch of people blocked the hallway. All their heads were hanging down, their backs slouching, arms dangling by their sides.

The team members formed up with guns raised. Pierce was ready to fire, but then his peripheral vision caught Captain Reynolds raising a hand.

"Wait! Hold your fire!" he commanded in a low voice. "Do not fucking shoot."

"Captain?" Lincoln asked.

The infected hadn't moved an inch, even as the torches danced across their faces. Alpha still had the element of surprise. If they shot, they'd lose it.

"Stay where you are." Reynolds broke into a careful stride forward.

"Captain," Pierce called out, but Reynolds ignored him.

Lincoln, Shepherd, and Murphy exchanged baffled and worried stares. What the hell was the captain planning?

Reynolds walked up to the closest infected. It was a young man with a goatee and mohawk. He definitely didn't belong to this school, so he must have wandered in at some point. Reynolds got way too close to him. Pierce gulped, his toes digging into the soles of his boots.

The captain flashed the torch into the mohawk guy's face. The blinding light should have made him flinch or blink or show some kind of reaction. There was none. Reynolds brought the barrel of the rifle forward and gently poked the mohawk guy's chest before retreating a step.

The infected slightly swayed backward. Pierce's finger was not on the trigger, but it was ready to move to it at the slightest sign of aggression from the hostiles. The mohawk guy stopped swaying and resumed standing in the same position, head down and all.

Reynolds backpedaled to the others, keeping his eyes trained on the infected as he beckoned his team by curling a finger toward himself.

"I think we can get through without fighting them," he said.

"Not a good idea, captain," Lincoln disagreed. "I say we smoke these fuckers."

"And alert the entire school and everyone in the vicinity outside? Not a chance."

"How do we even know it's safe?" Shepherd asked.

"They're unresponsive. All we gotta do is walk past them, and we're out of here." Reynolds pointed to the infected crowd. "The door is right there, just around the corner. We can't let this stop us."

"That's a lot of undead," Lincoln said.

Pierce couldn't help but notice how Lincoln constantly referred to them as "undead" even though that was technically incorrect. The people in front of them were very much alive, only infected.

"We'll just sneak past them. Try not to touch any of them, and we should be good."

"Should be," Lincoln said.

"There's no other way. We're doing this," Reynolds retorted, his nerves audibly frayed. "I'll go first. If any of them wake up, we shoot the fuck out of them and get out of here. Got it?"

Everyone nodded. Reynolds nodded back, and then he turned to face the death mob. He stopped in front of the mohawk guy as if waiting to confirm whether his theory about the infected being dormant was correct. When none of the hostiles showed signs of activity, Reynolds sidled into the crowd.

Pierce leveled the torch with the captain, following him with his gaze as he slunk deeper with each step he took. He wasn't going in a straight line. The infected were clustered far too close to each other at points, so he had to circumvent them.

Pretty soon, only shadows of Reynolds's movement could be seen, and then he was gone from view entirely, obstructed by the many infected.

"Did he make it?" Shepherd asked.

"Where the fuck is he?" Lincoln asked.

Seconds later, a beam of light behind the crowd pointed upward and flicked on and off a few times.

"I guess we're good to go. Who wants to go next?" Pierce asked. "Murph?"

"Nah, you guys go ahead. I'll watch your backs," Murphy said.

He tried to sound confident, Pierce noticed, but he was deathly scared. Completely understandable.

"I'll go," Shepherd said.

Just like Reynolds, she carefully dove into the crowd and crept past them.

"Easy for her. She's tiny," Lincoln said.

Less than a minute later, the flashlight on the other side of the crowd of infected clicked on and off again.

"Come on, Pierce," Lincoln said.

Pierce walked up to the mohawk guy. Only then did the putrid smell hit his nostrils. He sidestepped between mohawk guy and a woman facing away from him. He kept his rifle close to his chest as he moved step by step, his entire body tense.

The stench grew tenfold, and Pierce clamped his mouth shut to stop himself from coughing. It was the smell of pissed pants, fresh shit, rotten teeth, and dried blood. He held his gaze glued to the floor as he made the grueling walk. It felt like trying to balance a tightrope.

After what felt like minutes, he looked up. He still couldn't see the end of the crowd, but he also couldn't see Lincoln or Murphy, either. It occurred to him that he was surrounded by a lot of infected who stood inches from him. One wrong move and he'd be a dead man.

The thought was enough to cause panic to bubble inside Pierce's gut. In that instant, the easiest thing to do would be to throw the rifle in the air and barrel through the infected until he reached freedom.

Pierce closed his eyes and steadied his breathing.

Keep it together, Pierce. Come on. You got this.

He continued moving. Sounds of raspy breathing surrounded him, sometimes right in his ear. He ignored them as he moved on, trying not to think about what would happen if one of the infected came to life. The urge to spin frantically in order to keep all the hostiles in sight was strong, and the inability to move freely only added claustrophobia to the concoction already threatening to take control.

All kinds of people were here: young people, middle-aged people, old people, bulky people, thin people, uniformed people, civilians... All their heads hung down, steady breathing coming out of their mouths like someone sleeping peacefully.

Infected blocked his path. Two men pressed shoulder to shoulder, right in Pierce's way. He had to sidle all the way to the wall to find a gap in the crowd.

Pierce looked right and saw Shepherd and Reynolds standing close by, past just a few rows of infected. Shepherd was waving Pierce over, silently cheering him on. Seeing his two teammates and knowing the end was near greatly boosted Pierce's morale.

He let out the breath he hadn't realized he was holding as soon as he was in the clear. Never before had being able to move freely without people squeezing from all sides felt so good.

Holy fucking shit. Never doing that again, Pierce thought.

Reynolds clicked his flashlight on and off. Some time passed, and then Lincoln emerged from the group. He looked like he just finished walking in the park and not trying to maneuver his way past the infected.

Only one person remained. Reynolds signaled for Murphy to get moving.

One minute passed. Then two. Pierce and the others were starting to get worried. Reynolds nervously shifted from one foot to the other, his eyes scanning the crowd as if he was contemplating going into the crowd to retrieve Murphy.

But then movement came from the horde. Murphy appeared between two infected. The pace he was moving made them realize why it took him so long to show up. His steps were timid and small, barely inches of progress. His face was contorted into a grimace as if he was carrying a hundred pounds on his shoulders. His forehead, temple, and cheeks glistened with sweat.

Come on, Murphy.

Murphy stopped. His eyes met with the rest of the team. His chest heaved up and down. He looked like he was about to start crying.

"Come on, Murphy," Shepherd whispered.

Murphy continued moving. He grazed the hand of an infected. Pierce gripped his rifle firmly. Luckily, nothing happened. Murphy was really close. He stopped once again then closed his eyes while shaping his mouth in the letter O and exhaling like a pregnant woman going through labor.

Just a little longer, Murphy. Come on.

Murphy opened his eyes then took one wide step to the side. Even before his foot touched the ground, Pierce could tell that the outcome of it would be bad. It was like watching someone falling in slow motion and not being able to do anything about it.

Murphy's shoulder bumped into a woman facing away from him, sending her stumbling forward. It was a collision that easily could have been avoided, but Murphy must have been scared, eager to get the hell-walk over with as soon as possible.

The woman fell on another infected, which caused a domino effect of two other infected to totter to the ground. Everyone stood frozen, staring at the fallen infected.

It was a moment of anticipation; hoping that the gaffe would go unnoticed like a woman in the street standing up and continuing to walk after an embarrassing fall in uncomfortable heels.

Murphy's eyes were plastered to the toppled infected so intently that he hadn't noticed the zombie right next to him raising his head and opening his bloodshot eyes.

JAMES

James found that even putting distance to the restaurant didn't help eliminate the smell of death that permeated his nostrils. He kept looking back as if expecting Travis to be there, following them despite his head being split open.

"If this is a parasite, and we're all infected, then maybe we should get some antibiotics or deworming medication," Ricky said.

"We don't know what activates the parasite," Angela said. "For all we know, it's dormant inside us as we speak, and taking certain medications might trigger its awake."

"Why was Welco Labs even working on such a thing?"

"Beats me. Like I said, I'm just a cleaner there. The company daily introduces new drugs that they've developed. For all I know, that's what they were trying to do with this parasite."

"I don't see how a parasite could be used in a good way. I mean, what the fuck were they thinking using one for, anyway?"

"It's common in some countries. Some cultures deliberately infect themselves with tapeworms to lose weight."

"Disgusting."

James agreed with Ricky. It *was* disgusting. He couldn't stop his mind from conjuring an image of a long, wet, slithering worm poking out of a human ass. He almost gagged at the thought.

The revulsion was replaced by caution when a clipped scream erupted from somewhere. The high pitch of it told James that it was one of the infected.

"We'd best be quiet and keep an eye out," Angela said

They stopped talking after that.

More and more crashed cars riddled the street as they got closer to the city. The corpses were more numerous, too. James was a man who had always been sensitive to smells. Whenever he visited someone who used scented candles or air fresheners, he felt sick. That was why it surprised him that he was no longer aware of the stench of blood that surrounded him.

He assumed that his body was doing its part to protect him. The nose had grown accustomed to the smell until it could no longer differentiate it from fresh air.

When James looked up, the town's clock tower loomed in the distance. The tower, which also served as a town hall, was situated in the very center of the city, and it was visible from almost any location. When James first moved to Witherton, he used the clock tower as a landmark for orientation whenever he got lost.

Now, standing illuminated by floodlights against the dark sky, it looked like a sanctuary—a lighthouse in the middle of a stormy night.

James thought about the streets they'd need to cross in order to reach the clock tower. It would probably be impossible to reach it without attracting unwanted attention—provided that the streets were crossable at all.

But they weren't heading to the clock tower, he remembered then. That sent a pang of relief to loosen in his chest.

As they neared the intersection, Angela stopped. James almost bumped into her. At first, he thought she had seen something until he noticed the pensive look plastered on her face.

"What's up?" he asked.

She didn't answer for a few seconds. "Okay, if we take North Street and cut through… okay, yeah, that'll work."

"Want to share what you have in mind?" Ricky asked.

"Mapping the safest route in my head. Come on." She took two steps forward then stopped and turned to face Ricky and James. She had a serious look on her face; the look of a parent about to scold their child. "It's going to get really dangerous from here. Be really, *really* careful. All right?"

Both Ricky and James nodded. James felt the pocket of his pants to make sure the knife was still there. He gripped the hilt and pulled it out before shoving it back inside. Just testing to see how fast he could take it out. Hopefully, he was not going to be caught by surprise like with Travis.

Angela had been right. Now that they were near the epicenter, things were anything but quiet. James had half-expected the city to be like a warzone: gunshots, mixed screams, roaring engines of vehicles, sirens...

Despair flooded him when he realized that only the most undesirable sounds remained: The screams were coming from everywhere, bouncing from street to street, sometimes seemingly right above the group. Despite the animalistic grunts, screeches, coughs, and other sounds, they rang a certain docile note to them. These were sounds that the freaks made regularly, it seemed.

The reason why James was able to differentiate between them was because those ear-piercing squeals would occasionally puncture the air, which made the trio freeze until the sound receded. It was the sound of a new victim being spotted. In those moments, all James could do was remain entrenched in his spot and hope to God that the spotted victim in question was not him.

The gunshots were mostly gone. A very rare, distant *pop-pop* reverberated through the air, barely a whisper against the other sounds. It was all a symphony that sang about the infected ruling Witherton, all the normal people either dead or gone.

Angela was about to lead them into an alley when she quickly backed up behind the wall.

"Back, back," she whispered. "Three freaks in the alley. No way past them."

James was closest to the corner, so he dared to peek into the alley. It was dark, and the only thing he could see was the three stark figures standing still in the middle of the alley, heads and arms languidly hanging. The way they stood was enough to tell that they were infected. The spastic motion only solidified that belief.

"We'll go around," Angela said.

She slunk past the alley and then urged the other two to follow her. Ricky went next. Then it was James's turn. While crossing—and those two seconds felt like hours— he couldn't shake the feeling that the alley would suddenly explode with shrill cries as they spotted him.

But James was safely behind the wall on the other side without alerting the freaks, much to his relief. He hadn't realized until then that he was sweating from the tension despite the cold night.

Angela wasn't wasting time. She was already walking down the street, Ricky closely behind her. James sure as heck had no intention of falling behind. Not in this place.

Signs of struggle and killings were omnipresent, and it was like a war zone. Police and military vehicles were strewn around the streets, dead bodies of law enforcement and military personnel joining the civilians. The casualties were too great to count.

The dead bodies were hard enough to look at. Bullet holes, missing limbs, disfigured torsos and heads... James was glad that he hadn't been there to see it actually happening. But the really difficult part was staring at the children.

Every once in a while, James would see something that could cause him to jerk his head away immediately.

A tiny, blood-covered hand poking from under a tank; a small figure clutched in the arms of its dead mother; a stray shoe small enough to fit a toddler's foot...

James traced Angela's face for any reaction. Other than the concern that she'd been displaying this entire time, he couldn't read any emotions on her. He knew they were there, though. He didn't know how, but there was a subtle change about her that became discernible. No person, let alone a mother, could see something like this and stay indifferent.

"We can cut through here." Angela pointed toward an alley.

This one was clear of the freaks. The three still carefully tip-toed through the alleyway. James, who was at the back of the group, felt his muscles tensing up way too much as he looked behind every couple of seconds. They were in a narrow passage, and they could easily become surrounded. He tried to push that thought out of his mind as he sneaked behind Ricky.

Something caught his peripheral vision. Something in the dark that he shouldn't have seen in the first place but his brain decided to register nonetheless.

When James looked left, he could physically feel his blood running cold. A figure crouching by the wall was staring up at him. No fight or flight instinct was triggered in James. Instead, he remained frozen, staring at those bulbous eyes as they unblinkingly fixated on him.

The figure wasn't crouching. It was sitting by the trash container, the head slumping backward. Entrails were hanging out of the man's stomach, the guts spooling on and around his legs.

"Oh, fuck," James managed the word as he regained control of his body.

He almost let out a peal of laughter over his own ridiculousness.

"James?" Angela called from the front.

James snapped his head in her direction and then quickly averted it back to the dead body, out of fear that he would see it moving.

"Yeah. I'm coming." He nodded.

The fright made his legs feel like cooked noodles until the moment they stepped out of the alleyway. He needed a break, and he could see from the way Ricky's shoulders drooped that he wasn't the only one. Angela, on the other hand, seemed determined to continue going.

Ricky planted his palms on a parked and surprisingly intact Audi.

Then, the worst possible thing happened.

The car's alarm began blaring. Ricky backed away as if he had just touched a hot stove, his eyes wide in terror as his head swiveled from James to Angela. Angela had spun around, the ax firmly gripped and raised for an attack. She eyed Ricky, then the car, then Ricky again, in a look that said, "What did you do, you idiot?"

Then came the screams.

Oh, shit.

"Run!" Angela shouted, the word barely perceptible over the cacophony of noises that closed in on them.

She was running in one random direction. James was on autopilot when he began running after her. He was too focused on the death cries around him to worry about where she was going.

Soon, the first infected came into view. It was a completely nude man with a bloody stump for his hand. His eyes locked with Angela, and he broke into a sprint toward her. His penis swung like a pendulum between his legs as he dashed across the street, his mouth stretched open in a croaky scream.

He was about to collide with Angela when she stepped aside. The man hugged the air as he fell headlong, scraping his knees and elbows. But he was already clambering up to his feet, ready for round two. By then, Angela, Ricky, and James were already down the street.

More freaks emerged from adjacent streets and alleys, their heads jerking violently in both directions before locking with the targets. It was every man for himself now. James could only hope that the freaks would try to go after Angela since she was the fastest one.

Something grabbed his hand. James looked left to see an elderly woman tugging him backward, slowing him down. James had the bad luck of looking back and seeing the dozens of freaks that were closing in on him.

Shit!

"Let go!" He yanked, but the old woman's grip was too strong.

Only then remembering that he had a knife, he pulled it out of the pocket and swiped at the woman's wrist. A red line appeared on her forearm, and her bony fingers instantly released their grip on him. She looked surprised as she stared at her arm. By the time she locked eyes with James once again, he had already put twenty feet of distance between them.

He swerved between the infected that were too preoccupied with Angela to notice him until he brushed past them. By then, the screams were in his ears, followed by a stampede of footsteps. Any second, James expected a hand to close around his ankle, causing him to crash to the ground where the infected would pile on top of him and tear him to pieces.

His lungs were burning. His legs were burning. He desperately wanted to stop and smoke a cigarette. He wasn't sure how long he'd be able to run.

Angela ran across Chirp Park, past the statue dedicated to WW2 victims, and toward the cathedral. She was a solid hundred feet in front of Ricky and James, who were panting like dogs, trying to keep up with her.

"Shit! What's… she… doing?!" Ricky uttered.

James had no lung capacity to answer him. The freaks were coming from every direction, most of them still focused on Angela. She slowed down to cut one across the face with her ax before resuming the sprint. It still wasn't enough for Ricky and James to catch up to her.

When she ran up the stairs, James finally understood what Angela was trying to do—she was looking for refuge in the cathedral. She disappeared behind the pillars leading up to the cathedral, and that made James feel like he and Ricky were truly left to fend for themselves.

Some of the freaks followed Angela up the stairs before they, too, went out of view. Angela was done for, no doubt about it. James's eyes fell on the dark alley on the other side of the park. Running there and waiting for the dust to settle crossed his mind.

But, still on autopilot, he continued running toward the cathedral. Maybe he just didn't want to die alone. Maybe he still trusted that Angela wouldn't abandon them. Either way, he and Ricky somehow made it to the stairs without snagging any freaks along the way.

But then they ran into the ones that were standing guard on the stairs.

A young man in a Walmart uniform spread his arms and legs as he screamed at James. He then lunged forward. James ducked, but it was probably unnecessary because the man flew way above James before crashing head-first to the bottom of the steps. Even with all the drowning screams around, James heard the crack that had come from the young man's neck.

Another one stood in their way on the stairs, and he grabbed Ricky by the shoulders. The two spun in an unstable pirouette, looking like they were about to collapse together from the jerky movement.

James knew that man. Despite the grimace on his face, there was no mistaking that the person in question was James's coworker Zack.

"Stop!" James shouted as he made his way up the steps.

Zack was focused solely on Ricky. Ricky was the only person who existed in the world for him.

"Zack!"

Zack's eyes flitted to James. There was a moment of recognition in those eyes, a flicker of humanity. But just as quickly as it came, it was gone, and Zack was back to wrestling with Ricky.

His intention wasn't just to knock Ricky down. It was to kill him in the most violent way possible. And yet, as James stared at his lost coworker's eyes, he knew that it wasn't hate that was driving Zack. It was something far more primal than that, something akin to instinct. Maybe even instinct itself.

There was no saving Zack. No reasoning with him. James knew that when he beheld those bloodshot eyes.

He ran up the steps and, before he knew what he was doing, the knife in his hand was being plunged into Zack's neck.

Zack's eyes went wide, a gesture that must have mirrored James's own reaction. With the knife still stuck in his throat, his hands released Ricky and he stumbled backward. His heel awkwardly caught the edge of a step. His foot slipped, and then Zack was tumbling down the stairs. He crashed into one infected woman just as she began climbing the stairs, causing her to whack her face on the pavement.

When she looked up, her mouth was full of blood and chipped teeth. Only then did James's eyes fall on the myriad of people who were rushing toward the cathedral,

There must have been hundreds of them. All the way from the other side of the park, pouring from out of the alleys and nearby intersections, more and more kept congregating to the spot that had garnered so much attention.

"Move!" James urged Ricky, who seemed too transfixed on the freaks approaching the stairs.

They ran up the stairs. Angela was in front of the enormous wooden door, banging on it. Three corpses lay around her—belonging to the freaks that had run up after her just earlier.

"Come on! Open up!" she shouted as she rammed the door with her shoulder.

She turned around and raised her ax, her face rigid with anger.

"Whoa! Whoa! It's us!" James shouted.

Angela still raised the ax higher up and then brought it down at James. He ducked and instinctively closed his eyes. A crunching sound and a yelp above him later, he opened his eyes to see Angela's ax embedded in an infected person's face.

She pulled out the blade, and her victim fell like a ragdoll. James looked at the top of the stairs to see more of them coming. He rushed to the door, slamming his shoulder against it due to inertia. The ram did nothing to rattle the frame of the door, not even a bit.

This is it. It's all over, he thought to himself as he watched more and more figures rising from the staircase. Strangely, he thought of Julie in that moment. He couldn't help but wonder where she was, if she was okay, and, if she wasn't, whether her death was as painful and as riddled with fear as his would be.

The freaks were closing in. Ricky was backing up toward the door. Angela was holding her ax high above her head, her head darting from one freak to the other, trying to decide who she would attack first.

Then, the support on James's back was gone and he was falling backward. His back hit the floor hard, and he realized he was staring at a ceiling. When he raised his head, he realized that the door of the cathedral had been opened and that a figure stood above him.

"Hurry!" the person shouted as he motioned for Ricky and Angela to get in.

James scooted backward to give his companions space. He only vaguely realized that hands were grabbing him under his arm and pulling him deeper into the cathedral. Ricky barged in and collapsed on the floor. Angela had just finished pulling her ax out of an infected woman's chest.

And then she fell through the door as well. The person who had shouted at them to hurry grabbed the edge of the door with both hands and pushed it shut. Someone ran up next to him, carrying a big plank. They jammed the door with the plank just as a dull thud exploded on the other side, followed by a scream.

A series of bangs tore around the heavy door and walls of the cathedral, the screams overlapping and drowning each other out.

The two rescuers held the door braced while the bangs and screams slowly receded until they could be counted on the fingers of one hand.

Then, they stopped entirely, engulfing the interior of the cathedral in silence.

BEN

All Ben wanted was to get a weapon to defend himself, and he would be on his way. He didn't want to get into any fights with these people because they let him stay the night.

If he asked them to give him a gun, they most likely would have said no. Hell, he himself would have said no if he were in the same situation. Why give a gun to a stranger and risk the lives of your loved ones?

Loved ones, the phrase tasted bitter in his mind tonight.

Ben peeked out of the bedroom, and once he made sure the coast was clear, he tiptoed down the hallway and descended the stairs—slowly. Some of the wooden steps creaked, and he hoped the sound wouldn't wake anyone up.

The house was dark and quiet, but the distant popping and screaming could be heard outside, merely a lullaby. Ben dreaded seeing someone downstairs in the living room, but, to his relief, the couch was empty, no one in sight.

That's when he approached the first drawer and started rummaging through it. They had to have another gun somewhere in the house, maybe something small like a pistol. His assumption was only that—an assumption. If he didn't find any weapons—or other useful tools—he'd quietly exit the house, no big deal.

He opened every drawer below the vanity mirror but found nothing aside from hair products and useless papers. He was starting to lose hope.

The only remaining place he didn't search was the armoire. He approached it, feeling hopeful. He started by opening the bottom drawer. A smile crept up his face at the object that came into his view.

A revolver.

Ben took the gun in his hand, feeling its weight. It had been a while since he went shooting at the range, and he forgot how heavy pistols could be. He assumed the revolver was loaded due to its weight, and when he popped open the barrel, his assumption turned out to be true.

All six bullets sat in the chambers. Ben returned the barrel to its original position and felt around the drawer for any boxes of bullets. It wouldn't matter to the family if he took all the ammo with him. Not like they could use the caliber for their own guns.

Besides, Harry had a shotgun, and David—

"What do you think you're doing?" a deep voice cut through the air.

Ben's body jerked into an upright standing position, and before he knew what was going on, he was pointing the revolver at a darkened silhouette with a muscular outline.

The person reached to the side. A click later, the room was bathed in light, and Ben was standing in the middle of the living room, facing David.

The man's eyes flitted to the gun then up at Ben, reflecting a suspicious glower that said, *I fucking knew you'd be up to no good.*

"Answer me," David said.

He was wearing boxers and a wife-beater tank top.

Ben opened his mouth to explain himself, but the drumming of approaching footsteps distracted him. Harry and Martha raced down the stairs then froze when they saw Ben pointing the gun at David. Ben vaguely became aware that Harry's shotgun was in his hands—seriously, did he sleep with that thing?—and he knew that the possibility of him getting blasted was pretty high.

Blew their heads clean off, I did.

"I don't know what's goin' on 'ere, but I'm sure we can figure somethin' out," Harry said.

"I caught him going through your drawers," David said. "Look. He stole your gun."

"You put that gun down right now, mister," Martha said, venom in her eyes.

Ben was pointing a gun at her son-in-law, and that was unacceptable. Ben realized how bad it looked, pointing the gun at David, but it was too late now. The moment he lowered it, Harry would shoot him. That's what Ben would have done to a stranger pointing a weapon that belonged to him at one of his own people.

It was too late to back down.

"I don't want any trouble," Ben said.

"Neither do we, son. Let's talk 'bout this," Harry said.

But even as he said it, Ben could see his fingers turning white from how hard he gripped the shotgun.

"What's going on in here?" another voice joined in.

Caitlyn entered behind David. Her eyes searched the room and grew wide when she saw Ben with the revolver.

Great.

Immediately, David grabbed Caitlyn by the hand and pulled her behind himself, confirming Ben's assumptions that David was a selfless husband. Ben doubted he would have stood in front of Melissa to shield her from a man with a gun.

He only then remembered to look at David, to check if he had his pistol on him. His hands were empty, and he doubted David concealed a pistol in his boxers. Big mistake, coming to check what was going on in the living room without a firearm. He probably didn't think it was anything serious.

"What are you doing?" Caitlyn asked, her tone riddled with animosity toward Ben.

"Okay, listen," Ben said, raising his free hand up. "I just want the gun. I need it to defend myself, okay? I'm not gonna hurt anyone. I'm just gonna walk away, and none of us is going to get hurt. Sound good?"

"You say that while you're pointing your gun at one of our own. Harry, shoot the son of a bitch!" Martha hissed.

"Calm down, Martha. Son. Ben. Put the gun down," Harry said.

"I'm sorry. I can't do that."

"We let you in! We feed you dinner! We allow you to stay! And this is how you repay us?!" Martha screeched. "Harry, he's putting our children in danger! Kill him before he hurts one of them!"

Her overwrought behavior contrasted the jittery smoker attitude with the condescending smile she'd displayed earlier that day.

Ben turned to face David, who was scowling at him. Caitlyn was peeking over her husband's shoulder.

The periphery of Ben's vision caught movement. He turned his head and his gun, just in time for Martha to reach for Harry's shotgun.

Harry had been so focused on Ben that he noticed too late that his wife took the gun. Martha brought the stock of the gun to her hip and swiveled it. Her intention was clear, and Ben acted on survival instincts.

He pointed the revolver at her and squeezed the trigger.

A deafening bang came first. The second thing that came was the ringing in Ben's ears and then the screams. When Ben's brain processed what was going on, Martha was in a sitting position against the wall of the stairwell, eyes wide open, a smear of blood trickling from the wall above her where she hit her back.

Harry was standing next to her, wailing a long moan. Caitlyn was letting out caterwauls. And David…

Ben saw him dashing across the room toward him with the intention of tackling him. He whirled and fired another bullet. Another loud bang that momentarily silenced all the sounds in the room.

David's shoulder flinched, and he collapsed to the floor. He held a hand on the spot where he'd been shot, his face contorted in a rictus.

"No!" Caitlyn fell to her knees in front of him, holding him while looking up at Ben.

You fucking monster, that look said.

But she was wrong. Ben wasn't a monster. This was just a misunderstanding. He just wanted a gun, and no one would have gotten hurt. This was Martha's fault. She was the real monster here.

The heat of the moment reminded Ben that he'd shot Martha, so he looked toward her to confirm whether she was dead or not. Harry was kneeling next to her, wailing as he held one blood-covered hand on her belly, the other on her cheek, telling her to wake up. His fingers left bloody smears on her face.

She's dead. I killed her. This was my doing.

Ben couldn't tell how long they all stood in those positions, frozen, but he became aware of the pain in his shoulder from holding the gun raised the whole time. It was the sounds outside that snapped him out of his stupor.

Someone was banging on the door and had been doing so for the past few minutes. Ben sneaked a glance but couldn't see anything from where he was standing. The muffled growls and the groans that came from the other side of the door told him what he feared.

"You lured them here," Caitlyn said.

Shit. They must have heard the gunshots and would come down on the house like lions on their prey. This place was no longer safe, and Ben needed to get out.

Caitlyn was still kneeling above David. He still held a hand on his bleeding shoulder, and his painful facial expression was now mixed with a hint of hate. Harry stopped moaning, and his hand slowly inched toward the shotgun near Martha's feet.

"Don't," Ben commanded, pointing the gun at Harry. "I don't wanna do this. I didn't want to hurt anybody."

Harry's hand retreated, and he resumed sobbing over his wife's dead body. Thirty-five years of marriage snuffed out by a single bullet. All Ben's doing.

"I'm gonna fucking kill you." David groaned.

It made Ben want to blow his head off. But he didn't because he didn't want to cause any more damage to the family than he already had. And because he needed the bullets.

"I'm sorry. I never meant for any of this to happen," Ben said as he backpedaled to the front door.

He had no idea what he was doing. He just wanted out of that house and to never see the accusatory faces that stared at him.

"I'm sorry," he said again.

His heel bumped against the door. The loonies, as Harry and Caitlyn called them, were just on the other side of the door. Mere inches of wood separated Ben from certain doom. But his escape was over there, too.

One hand intermittently pointed the gun between Harry and Caitlyn, the other fumbling to reach for the lock on the door.

"No. Don't do it," Caitlyn said. "You're gonna get us all killed. Just stop. Please."

But Ben wasn't listening. He needed to get out of there immediately. He couldn't bear to be in this house a moment longer with the body of the woman he just killed and the man he injured. Taking his chances with the loonies was a preferable option.

"I'm sorry," he said once more before turning the lock and stepping aside.

The moment seemed to last an eternity.

Then, the door burst open with such intensity that it almost smacked Ben in the face. The first of the loonies dashed inside. Ben watched as Caitlyn's eyes grew wide, as she held a hand out in front of herself in a useless attempt at defense, as the loony crashed into her, pushing her onto her back.

Then another stepped in. And another.

The open door concealed Ben enough for the loonies to focus on the other survivors in the room. One fell on top of David. The other went after Harry, he assumed. But he couldn't see it.

He wasn't thinking when he went around the door and barreled outside. He sprinted as more throaty cries of the monsters approached the house. He heard gunshots then a blood-curdling scream that pierced through every other sound.

By the time Ben stopped behind a house to catch his breath, the only sound was his own, heavy panting. He leaned on his knees, focused on breathing, but he couldn't get the image of the bullet he fired going through Martha's chest.

The way she stumbled backward, the way her head jerked back as if electrocuted, the way her arms flew sideways and the shotgun dropped from her hands like a hot potato, the way the exit wound on her back left a smear on the wall that trickled down along with her as she slid into a sitting position.

Nausea rushed from Ben's stomach into his throat.

He puked out the lasagna he had for dinner all over the grass. Water and chunks of meat flew out of his mouth, burning his throat. Three waves of vomit came out, and then he dry-retched twice before the reflex went away.

Jesus. That was close. I could have died. What if I ran straight into the arms of one of those things? How close had I come to dying? Had I stayed just a few seconds longer...

Staring down at his trembling knees and hands, Ben noticed the revolver still in his hand. He'd been clutching it this entire time on autopilot. A part of him wanted to throw it away because it was a murder weapon.

No, he would never do that, no matter how bad the weapon was. He needed it. But he also needed to find a reason as to why things happened in the house the way they did.

He wasn't a murderer. He shot Martha and David in self-defense. That was all. Martha was going to shoot him. It was either him or her. He didn't want to do it. And if he hadn't shot David, he would have wrestled the revolver out of his hand, and then what? Then he'd shoot Ben just as Ben shot Martha.

It was self-defense. And the other deaths? It was the loonies, not him. The more Ben told himself that, the more he believed it. Maybe his brain was just looking for a defense mechanism. He didn't care. He refused to accept the responsibility for that family's death.

Would the police see it that way, though? Harry's words echoed in Ben's head, *Even the poh-leece can't do nuffin' about it.*

Laws no longer existed in Witherton, apparently. A terrifying, but equally exhilarating realization crossed Ben's mind as he stared at the revolver. He indirectly got an entire family killed, and he wouldn't answer for that. No one would.

He had more important matters to worry about. He had to find a way out of Witherton.

And now that he had a gun, he'd feel a lot safer looking for an exit.

THE END

Boris Bacic

INFECTED CITY

Book 1: Emergency Broadcast
Book 2: Necrotic Streets
Book 3: Quarantine Terror
Book 4: Decaying Haven
Book 5: Outbreak Chaos
Book 6: Dead End

Printed in Great Britain
by Amazon

23862989R00092